"Mike Weiss' novel marks the debut of a new series. . . . If Weiss can maintain the wry charm and freshness exhibited here, the prospect pleases."

San Diego Union

"This novel makes good use of its San Francisco setting and the author's ability to instill logic into a complex plot."

Newsday

"A tough, entertaining mystery."

San Jose Mercury News

"Weiss has a brisk, snappy, wisecracking style that keeps the plot from dragging. . . . Ben Henry gets a big tip from this reviewer."

Des Moines Sunday Register

"The taxi-driver angle gives Weiss the opportunity to explore San Francisco streets and capture the back-seat vignettes of riders seen through Henry's rear-view mirror. . . . Weiss writes with verve and zest."

The Washington Post

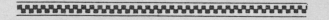

NO GO ON JACKSON STREET

A BEN HENRY MYSTERY

Mike Weiss

FAWCETT CREST • NEW YORK

Harry and Josh, my father and my son.
And for C.L.

1

It was slow, as Sunday nights usually are. I nosed the taxi through the darkened streets of the Mission district looking for a flag, considering the possibility of still another burrito supper while I listened to Doris croon intersections on the dispatch radio. "Gold and Montgomery," she called in her juicy-fruit tone. "Fell and Divisadero, Sunnydale and Schwerin, Twenty-ninth and Mission. Let's pick up these orders before they're cold, drivers. KYA 894, the Checker Cab time is nine forty-five." Some choices: a graybeard bar, a nasty housing project, and one call that might be a residence but more likely was a phone booth. Twenty-ninth and Mish was the only call close enough to check in on, but it was too far to ride to help somebody carry home their groceries from the Safeway. As I drove I did the quick, habitual arithmetic that was as much a part of driving taxi as pushing down on the accelerator and the brake pedal until the blackened heel of your right shoe literally wore away; I concluded, as I had at six o'clock, and seven, and eight, that at my current pace I'd end the night taking home barely enough to make the ten-hour shift worthwhile. The music of Turk Murphy, broadcasting live from the New Orleans Room of the Fairmont Hotel, kept me bouncing along in a reasonable mood. I couldn't handle another burrito after all and decided instead to slide on down toward City Hall and see if I could make it to McDonald's before ten o'clock closing.

Doris called the board again. "Gold and Montgomery, Fell and Divis—anybody for the Western?—Sunnydale and Schwerin with a phone number, Twenty-ninth and Mish before her ice cream melts, Sixteenth and Albion." Sixteenth and Albion was probably the bar at the lip of the alley, but it was only two blocks away. I was into my wide, illegal U-turn before she finished talking, snatching my microphone off its hook with my other hand. Round, round, I get around: Jay and the Americans? Neil Diamond? Who could remember? Somebody honked to object to my turn but I was already speeding east on Sixteenth Street, a shadow of regret for the french fries I wouldn't be eating passing over my appetite. Doris checked two other drivers while I accelerated through a changing yellow light to pull up outside the bar just as she told me to pick up the call. I jammed the cab into parking gear, hit the blinkers, and headed toward the bar. Before I reached the door two other Checkers rode by one after another to see for themselves that I hadn't stretched and was really closer to the call than they were. Three cabs reaching a crummy bar call inside of one minute—that was about as slow as a night could be short of nuclear wipeout. Well, there would be drivers who would work right through a Russian missile attack; some wise guys looking for an angle were sure to decide there'd be a lot of people wanting to leave town.

The saloon was one of those bereft little places with the television running but the sound off, Tex-Mex on the juke-box, and mostly empty stools at the bar. Just breathing the air could make you woozy. "Taxi," I said loudly from the doorway, pausing only long enough for the bartender to acknowledge me, nod toward a guy with a Bud in front of him, and say, "He'll be right out." I went back behind the wheel and waited impatiently for my load while Turk and the boys played their last licks down at the Fairmont, where waiters were serving the drinks in clean glasses and wiping out the ashtrays and the room smelled of money in the form of perfume and aftershave.

When I saw the way my load walked out of the bar I sighed. He was blindly purposeful, brushing the doorway and then a lamppost on his way toward my taxi. "Where you headed?" I asked him when he climbed in the back. In the glow of the interior light when he opened the cab door I got a good look at him and he wasn't dangerous, just an old Mexican with leathery skin and iron-filing hair whose obsidian eyes were quietly, thoroughly stoned. It might be okay.

He smiled. I smiled back. He said nothing. "Where to?" I asked. Silence. "You going home?" He nodded. That was progress, I supposed. "Where you want me to take you?"

"Mi casa."

"Where d'ya live?" At that point I punched the meter. I could taste the large order of french fries I had passed up for this opportunity to serve the public.

"Hokay, mi casa." He smiled again.

"You gotta tell me where; how'm I gonna take you there otherwise?"

"Hokay."

"Not okay. *Á donde?*" It was never a good sign when I had to resort to my pidgin Spanish. Could be worse, though, like the three belligerent Polish merchant sailors.

"Dayses."

"Texas?"

"*Si, si,* dayses."

"Texas Street on Potrero Hill? You gotta tell me, hombre. I don't have all night." The meter clicked.

"No, no. Dayses ee gare."

Oh, sweet Jesus. "Un momento," I told him. I grabbed my pen and ripped a sheet off the pad I always carried. "Escribe," I said, handing them to him. Doris was calling addresses where they wanted taxis; the night had abruptly woken up. There was a call near Dolores Park and another one even closer on Liberty Street. Nice middle class residences. I imagined lonely beautiful women, or quiet people going to the airport to catch the red-eye East. Arduously my guy was writing on the paper, first having licked the point of my felt-tip pen, leaving an ink stain on his tongue. He was frowning with concentration. Wobbly block figures were making their way onto the paper one at a time. 1 6 G U R A R A.

"Sixteenth and Guerrero. Diez y seis y Guerrero, si? You know that's only two blocks from here?"

"Hokay," he said.

A driver named Jimmy the Glove told the story of how, under similar circumstances but with a passenger whose fat roll of bills was overflowing his pocket, he watched the guy fall asleep in his back seat, hit the meter, parked the cab, went into a bar, and drank and rolled liar's dice until closing time, before driving the john the one block he wanted to go. He collected the ninety bucks on the meter plus a ten dollar tip the guy threw him for getting him home safely. No such luck for Ben Henry. I drove mine to 16th and Guerrero, a buck seventy on the meter. "Here you go," I said, just glad to be rid of him.

"No."

"Whattaya mean, no?"

"Dayses ee gare."

"This is it, here." I showed him the piece of paper and then pointed at the street sign. "See, Sixteenth and Guerrero." Some other taxi had already picked up near Dolores Park, the Liberty Street call was gone too, and the dispatch radio was quiet again. Turk Murphy was off the air, a few cars swished by, but the sidewalks were empty and McDonald's was closing.

"No." He looked stubborn. He didn't budge.

That was it. "Out!"

"No."

"*Si.* " I was out from behind the wheel in no time flat and around to the curbside passenger door. I took hold of his arm and began to pull. He was just a little guy with a spindly arm, but he resisted with a stubborn strength. I had to pry his fingers loose, not knowing whether to hit him or cry in frustration. It was a struggle, but I finally managed to deposit him on the sidewalk—collecting the fare was out of the question—and drive away. I looked over my shoulder and saw him still sitting there on the sidewalk in the pool of light cast by a street lamp. Now that I was clear of him I realized he was just the sort who would carry a wicked pocketknife.

I used to be slow to burn, but the frustrations of the taxi had shortened my fuse to a dangerous length. If he had gutted me, would there have been an obituary in my old newspaper? Who needed this? I mean, how had I become someone who threw drunks onto the sidewalk?

I needed to cool out, so I grabbed a doughnut and a coffee with nondairy creamer—every American's fair share of daily carcinogenic—over on Castro Street. Somebody was waiting beside my cab when I came out, so I munched and sipped on the move with the meter running, which instantly improved my spirits. I dropped him and lit a cigarette and finished my coffee and was flagged down right away and was back in business. Doris went off the air just before eleven and was replaced by Andy, who sounded like he had a hangover but gave me a pickup right away. My mood evened out as long as the cab was occupied. They say the customer is always right, but only customers believe it. From behind the wheel it's the meter that's always right.

Down near Union Square, which was deserted at that hour except for the lumps of humanity who had settled down to sleep on the park benches and a trio of streetwalkers strolling by the brightly lit display window of Saks looking worn in contrast to the mannequins, I was hailed by a man wearing what Herb Caen called a full Cleveland—doubleknit polyester, white belt, and white shoes. The rube held the door open for his wife, who slid into the back seat with a rush of perfume.

"How's it goin', fella?"

"Not bad. Where to?"

"You know the Seascape Motel on Lombard Street?"

"Seascape," I said, and punched the meter. I didn't know the place, but I'd spot it once I hit the motel strip on Lombard.

As I was shooting out Geary past the darkened theaters he said, "We're in a rush, fella. Get us there fast and I'll take good care of you." His wife giggled inexplicably.

The ones who say they'll take care of you are all stiffs, but maybe he'd be an exception. As for *fast*, I get everybody there fast. When the rides were coming quick and steady the taxi's big V-8 became an extension of my wits, and I was more deft and certain than I had ever been at a typewriter. What a thing to be good at. I caught the synchronized green lights on Pine Street and began my run along the lower edge of Nob Hill, hurtling past the apartment building where the French chef with the Japanese name had been murdered, cruising at a steady fifty through Polk Gulch, where I swerved around two drag queens taking their time crossing against a red light, coming as close to hitting them as I possibly could. *Olé.*

"Whatever you do, don't die in California," he was saying in the back seat. "If you get terminally ill you move to Utah, see? You'll save your estate a bundle." There was a call on the dispatch radio at Lombard and Broderick, and I listened carefully. If nobody took it the second time it was called, I could check in en route and the dispatcher would hold it until I got there.

"Really?" she said. I glanced in the rearview. She was dyed blonde, no longer young, heavily made up with ostentatious earrings and a lot of perfumed cleavage. "I didn't know about that, Charlie. That's good advice to know about." It sounded like she wasn't his wife after all, and that accounted for why she had giggled when he said, "We're in a rush." Love in the night—well, coitus in the dark, anyhow.

"I made some bad investments, Charlie. I don't know how to say no to a friend, if you know what I mean."

"Whatever." Sympathetic fellow, Charlie.

"I mean, I'm just seeing the light at the end of the tunnel, and I'm thinking about municipal bonds for my future."

I was on Lombard now, flashing past restaurants, neon-lit motels, gas stations, flying right along while my eyes automatically swept the sidewalks for anyone flagging a taxi. All of a sudden I saw their motel and jammed the cab abruptly into an opening in the traffic lane to my right, cutting off a driver who had to step on his brakes. He hit his highbeams to show his disapproval.

"Well, listen, all I can tell you is dying in California will cost you beaucoup bucks."

I reached Charlie's motel in under five minutes, a great crosstown run. Would Charlie show his appreciation? Would the Giants win the pennant? There was $4.70 on the meter when he helped her out and handed me a ten. I counted out a quarter and a nickel and then five singles so he'd have a buck in his hand for my tip. He looked down at his palm, removed the nickel, and handed me back the quarter.

"You're really reckless, you know that, fella?"

A quarter. He had taken good care of me all right. I pulled away without really looking, and behind me somebody honked his horn with displeasure. What was I doing abusing my dignity for quarters? Bad recollections dropped over my thoughts like a heavy stage curtain. I remembered Mazer, the managing editor, telling me just what the publisher thought of me the afternoon when he fired me and I walked out of *The Courier* building for the last time. Now here I was in a position where a guy in white shoes whose best advice to his date was to drop dead in Utah could tip me twenty-five cents, and worse, make me angry by doing it. Fifty cents would have been a lousy tip too, but it wouldn't have twisted my mood up like a junker in the grip of a metal crusher. So how I felt could be altered by two bits. A quarter. A peepshow cost fifty cents and a candy bar thirty-five. What could you buy with a quarter? Answer: *The Courier. The Courier* was the only thing in town that could be had for a quarter. *The Courier*, and Ben Henry's goat.

I took my roll out to count it: lousy. The count was a form of poison on a bad night, and so were the bills themselves. The Environmental Protection Agency said dollar bills were toxic. Maybe the EPA had been bought off by the banks who wanted cash outlawed and credit cards in every pocket. The hell with it. I was hungry, and Clown Alley just across the street served a decent hamburger fast enough not to cost me too much time.

When the grillman flipped my burger, grease dripped onto the hot coals, a flame shot up sizzling, and my empty stomach grumbled approvingly. I carried my white paper

sack outside when the hamburger was ready and ate behind the wheel listening to the dispatch radio. Juices rolled
down my hand and onto my wrist and I dabbed at them
with a napkin, but I couldn't wipe away the feel of greasy
residue on my skin. Just as I was prying the lid off the
coffee, Andy called a Jackson and Spruce on the radio.
Some instinct told me that even though I was pretty far
away nobody else was going to take the call, so I started
the motor and sluiced into traffic, momentarily forgetting
the coffee, which sloshed over my lap. I brushed ineffec-
tually at the pool of hot coffee and checked in at the same
time. But you meet a lot of interesting people, don't you?

Andy said, "Six two six, you get 3670 Jackson."

Driving fast uphill into Pacific Heights I wiped the seat
dry as best I could with my pocket handkerchief, tightened
the lid on the remaining coffee that hadn't spilled, tossed
the greasy sack and the sodden napkin into the street, and
tried to see an address as I wheeled onto Jackson Street.
The 3600 block had big homes along both sides, big brick
and stone houses with trees out front so old the Franciscan
fathers might have lifted their cassocks under them. I knew
that 3670 would be just beyond the middle of the block on
the north side. I left the motor running and climbed the
stone steps that wrapped around a parapet with the address
carved into it. I peered through a triple-width door of thick
glass and wrought iron. Electric lamps made to resemble
gas fixtures were mounted on either side. There were no
lights lit inside the house. I rang the bell and waited.

The street was night quiet. From the open window of my
cab the dispatcher's litany sounded like a parrot squawking
several rooms away. Nothing stirred on Jackson Street except
the breeze through the trees making a dry rustle. It had been
an unusually warm summer following a dry winter, and a
drought had leeched hold of Northern California. They were
already rationing water in Marin County, proving once again
that the rich always suffered worst. When I pressed the bell
a second time it chimed loudly, but still nobody came. It was
starting to look like a no-go. I pressed my nose to the glass
but couldn't see much of anything. The place felt empty of

human habitation. I went back down to my taxi, which hummed and throbbed at the curb.

"Checker six two six," I said into my hand mike. "Over."

"Who's that over?" Andy asked.

"Six two six over."

"Six two six?"

"The Jackson Street is a no-go."

"You certain, Ben? That was fresh when you took it. Lady said she needed a cab right away."

"Nobody here now, Andy."

"Okay, sorry. Got nothing else close to you." He paused and then said, "KYA 894, the Checker Cab time is midnight straight up."

You got no-gos almost every night—prank callers, or people who called and then changed their mind and didn't answer the door, or who gave you a mistaken address—but the drunken old man, the rube with the quarter, the wet front of my pants where the coffee had spilled, and the no-go were enough for one night. I was exhausted, used up, and nasty spirited, and working another hour would just make it worse. There was the usual throbbing pain deep inside my right thigh and the back of my neck was knotted tighter than the suspension coils on the Golden Gate Bridge. What in God's name was I doing playing at the nickel-dime-and-quarter table? Even Mazer acknowledged that I was a good reporter when he canned me for the publisher. "But talent isn't what makes or breaks you in our business," he said. "You require discipline."

"Know where I can get some cheap, Mazer?"

He shook his head, "It's not your newspaper. It's not mine either. It's Mr. Thiesmann's. What's the use, you don't want to understand, do you?"

A couple of young sports in blazers ran out of a fancy-dancy saloon on Union Street trying to flag me down, but my head was spinning and I drove right by them heading back to the yard. Their arms were both raised when I passed them, like a Dadaist deodorant commercial. No matter how fast I moved in the taxi I never got anywhere.

2

The man in the back seat wore a turban. He was poking a snub-nose revolver into my shoulder blade, making it hurt. I wanted him to stop but I couldn't wriggle free. The cab was filling up with briny water and my lap was wet. I tried to call for help but each time I started to talk into the mike I pushed the meter by mistake and numbers swam across its digital face in rapidly changing nonsense patterns. There was an insistent ringing. I rose desperately through the water toward the surface, my lungs heaving like stevedores in August. The telephone was ringing.

"Hullo." I said it loud and hearty to make whoever was on the other end believe I was wide awake and raring to go. It didn't fool her. Very little I did ever had, though when there had still been hope for the marriage she had pretended not to see or understand the things that hurt her most.

"Can't you get out of the sack long enough to send me my check?" No preliminaries. "Today's the fifth of the goddamn month and the mortgage is overdue. You know?"

I tried to talk but nothing came out except for a slurry croak. I cleared my throat.

Lottie was silent, and her silence was a catalog of recriminations. It spoke of every nook and fold of disappointment and of everything I had walked away from when I had left her. Ah hell, maybe it didn't say a word. Maybe

10

that was my rabid conscience chasing its own short tail. If I had ever known for certain what her silence signified, maybe things would have been different. More probably not, though.

Softly I said, "All right, Lottie, I'll get a check in the mail today. I'm sorry." I swung my size thirteens over the side of the bed and sat up, rubbing my chest to ease the ache near my breastbone. My place overlooked the intersection of Broadway and Columbus. Behind me and out of sight was Chinatown. In front of me was North Beach, its landscape outside my skylight dominated by strip joints. Carol Doda's place was diagonally across Broadway. Back when North Beach had still been a decent place, a 300-pound press agent for the nightclubs named Davey Rosenberg had noticed a newspaper photo of a topless bathing suit created in Paris by Rudi Gernreich. Inspired, Rosenberg bought a bikini bottom for a waitress and put her on stage in it that night. Naturally he had informed both the cops and the press. The rest was all flashing neon mammaries and drunken tourists. From the angle at which the sunlight was falling on Ms. Doda's blinking pink nipples, it appeared to be midmorning.

"Can I rely on *that*?" Lottie asked.

Now it was my turn to be silent. Like two boxers who wouldn't stop trading blows even after the final bell had rung and all the customers had gone home, we were playing to an empty house. "I do have recourse, you know," she said. I started to respond but she slipped the punch by hanging up before I could get it out. I was left with a dial tone and, mysteriously, the smell of her talc in my nostrils.

I massaged my right thigh where it still ached from pushing a gas pedal and then transferred my attention to my stiff neck and shoulders, aware of the softness of my skin. I had been told by a woman whose name I couldn't any longer remember that I had very soft skin for a strong man, and it was one of those casual things said in an idle moment that had remained embedded in self-consciousness long after the person who had said it had been lost. At the back of my neck the hair was as thick as wisteria on a

Savannah veranda. Time for a haircut. I put the old white enamel kettle up to boil and padded downstairs to collect the morning paper from where the kid left it just inside the street-level door. The stairwell was painted fire engine red with lime trim: Chinese landlord. I felt like garbage the way I usually did the night after I drove a taxi. Still bleary, I tossed the paper onto the table, having only noticed a headline at the bottom of the front page about a forest fire burning near Napa Valley. Either there wasn't much real news or Mazer hadn't liked the news there was.

In the bathroom I examined myself in the mirror and considered shaving. Since I had started driving taxi I had developed small but noticeable sag lines under my eyes. The eyes were the same, pale green and widely spaced around a tomahawk nose, but I wondered if I was taking on that worn look so many cab drivers had. A lot of them looked like aged boys, used but not experienced.

Beyond a certain age, an age I had passed, a man was responsible for his own face. A young man's self-scrutiny was merely vanity. At my age looking at yourself in the glass was a perilous exercise in character assessment. The hell with shaving, I was already tired of looking at myself. I settled for a hot shower and a brisk toweling.

When I was dry I went to the safe, which was cleverly disguised as a dresser drawer full of underwear and socks, and counted out what I had to send to Lottie. Then I counted what remained. Not enough and just enough, same old story. If you took into account that what the IRS didn't know didn't hurt me, I was actually doing better driving taxi than I had as a reporter. Well, what did it matter? It was not as if I could work at *The Courier* again. Thiesmann had fired me from the only job I ever really wanted for the grievous error of doing my job too well.

Sipping my first cup of coffee I shook a cigarette loose and lit up. As I inhaled, a hacksaw swept across my lungs. I really had to cut back. My stomach greeted the coffee by drowning it in juices as pleasant as a plumber's handkerchief. I pulled the sports section out of the paper—it was printed on green paper, maybe because it was a moneymaker—and found that the Giants had lost to the Braves in Atlanta again. When I finished with the sports section and the obituaries, I went back to the front page. There were two stories above the fold. The pound had improved against the dollar, but that concerned me about as much as a resumption of the Boer Wars would have. The other story, under a six-column headline, was more interesting.

The gossip columnist for the afternoon paper, *The Bulletin*, who was the city's most widely read newspaperman besides being its most influential boulevardier—I knew more than one man whose ambition was to be Harry Shugart's idea of a San Francisco guy—had been murdered in his home. There was a photo of a bunch of cops milling around in front of a stone parapet while the body bag was wheeled toward an ambulance on a gurney. I recognized the parapet, and if you looked very closely you could see the address carved into it: 3670. My no-go on Jackson Street. It gave me a peculiar feeling, a kind of tug, not of sorrow for Harry, but of involvement. I scanned the story rapidly until I found that the coroner had set the time of death at between 11 p.m. and 2 a.m. I had expected that because of the familiar tug.

Harry was—had been—a very neat, well packaged man who laughed a lot but with no particular warmth. He had sandy, kinky hair and a widow's peak and the rosy complexion of somebody who both drinks and exercises. His nose was his most prominent feature, a bright and bulbous ornament. He wore starched collars that always looked a tad too tight to be comfortable. But Harry would have been uncomfortable unless he was turned out just so. What saved Harry from appearing comical was his bearing, his success, and the shrewdness in his eyes.

In his daily column, which he had been writing for maybe forty years with no loss of bite or vigor, Harry Shugart had tossed off acute observations, sly witticisms, and out-of-school tattle about the prominent and the ordinary as easily and even more entertainingly than Nixon told lies. He was the best damn reporter in San Francisco, and he often scooped the city desk. He was also a masterful stylist, maybe the best anywhere at catching the pulse of his city—and by depicting it, creating it, so that life there began to imitate his imitation—since Runyon. His own obituary for himself would have been better than anything *The Courier* had produced to mark his passing. Reading Harry Shugart was as much part of San Francisco life as cracked crab and corrupt cops, and many people didn't pass a day without saying, "Did you see in Harry Shugart's column how . . ." Of course Harry also knew when to keep his typewriter silent—I had always admired him for sticking to his old typewriter when the computer system was installed—and his judicious silences were the real source of his power, which was considerable, as great as Winchell's in his day in New York. Harry Shugart was a powerful man because everybody talked to him, and he had become not only the city's chronicler laureate but also the walking repository of San Francisco's best secrets.

He had made reputations and fortunes, had ended promising careers, and had sharpened the ellipsis into something lethal. Harry Shugart had a thousand conspicuous friends and uncounted silent enemies, only now it sounded as if one of his enemies had finally . . . spoken.

3

"Hi there," he said, when I answered the phone. "You recognize the voice?"

"Sure, it's Ralph Edwards. What are we playing, This Is Your Life? C'mon, Y—"

"Names aren't necessary."

"Is that a phenomenological observation?"

"Truly. I'd like to talk to you if that's not inconvenient."

"Have you eaten breakfast?"

"My dear Benjamin, it's barely noon. Is Enrico's in thirty minutes satisfactory? I've got an item that might be of interest."

"Do I get a clue?"

"You just did, Sleuth."

"Don't call me that, Yollo." The offhand reminder of Buddy, Buddy alive and Buddy dead, shook me. "Only Buddy ever called me that."

"Enrico's in thirty then?"

"Okay."

"Cross carefully," he said, and the line went dead.

I dressed in my most comfortable clothes, worn jeans and a well traveled English-made pale yellow shirt open at the collar, my calf-high Italian boots that I felt called upon to tell people were *not* cowboy boots, and the Danish chamois sport coat with the burgundy silk lining that

15

fit me better than anything else I had ever worn, its drape a perfect complement to my own loose-jointedness. It was hanging in the wardrobe next to Buddy's black mohair suit, one of only two things I had taken as keepsakes of his existence, the other being his copy of *The Count of Monte Cristo*. Why'd you cut out on me, Buddy?

The lining around the inside breast pocket of my jacket was frayed because I always clipped my pen to it. I never went anywhere without my pen and a plain brown pad about five inches high bound with black tape. It was getting hard to find the pads; in the whole city only Patrick's down on Market Street still stocked them and I went down there regularly, always on foot, to replenish my supply, usually stopping as well at the tobacconist where I picked up a few of H. Upmann's short Coronas out of the humidor room and a tin of little Dannemans off the rack. The Dannemans and my cigarettes I put into a side pocket of my jacket along with matches. Finally I slipped on my sunglasses and did as Yollo instructed, crossing first Columbus and then Broadway, stopping momentarily to look over the magazine rack in the store that sold periodicals and dildos, cigarettes, candy, newspapers, and vibrators, and which, while it surely had a name, was known merely as the dirty newsstand.

I took a table on the patio at Enrico's facing the street. Yollo arrived a few moments later on Buddy's bike. For a dealer and a jack of many illicit and illegal trades, subject to the usual bouts of uncontrollably malevolent paranoia, he did not maintain what the ad boys call a low profile. Fat people are conspicuous to begin with and the quite short and very fat more so. When somebody is quite short and very fat and has a jet black beard with a white streak down its middle like a skunk, he sticks out in a crowd, especially when wearing a chartreuse jumpsuit with a large brass buckle hitched over a belly that crests like a plump capon stuffed with truffles and wild rice. Should none of this arouse any curiosity it helps to arrive on a Harley 850 and to demonstrate superhuman strength by lifting the bike onto the sidewalk with an unstrenuous jerk and to lock it

to the pole of a red and white no-parking sign. At the end
of this little performance in the art of remaining incon-
spicuous I was the only person on the busy patio not wondering who he was, and that was merely because I knew
Mr. Yollo Current.

He waddled across to my table, leaning on a walking
stick. "Let's take one in the corner, shall we?" he said.

I followed him to a table between a pillar and a wall
partially hidden from the street by a potted palm. He was
carrying an expensive leather satchel on a shoulder strap,
which he set down carefully between his feet before he
picked up his menu. He studied the menu silently while I
waited, knowing better than to try to get his attention when
he was considering what to eat. Finally he ordered three
eggs, home fries, toast, a double rasher of bacon, half a
cantaloupe, and a cappuccino. The waiter was just a kid.
He wore tight black leather pants. His hair was dyed yellow on one side and napalm orange on the other.

"How do you want those eggs?" he asked.

"Crisp at the edges and loose in the yolk," Yollo said.

The waiter hesitated, looking perplexed. It made my
day to see somebody with two-tone hair confused by an
order of eggs. Finally the puzzlement lifted from his un-
finished face. "Over," he said. "You want them over."

Yollo gave him a look of disdain that would have dev-
astated anybody brighter. "I asked for them crisp at the
edges and loose in the yolk. Can I make it any plainer
than that?"

The kid jotted something on his pad, took my order,
and retreated.

"Youth today." Yollo sighed. He was probably only a
few years older than the waiter, but he had been born old.
His eyes were small and set deep in protective folds.

Yollo had been the ward, in a manner of speaking, of
the only real friend I have ever known, Dr. Bertram Allen
Singer, Buddy. Buddy was the first and last man I knew
who wanted nothing and so had everything. Many people
must have found him abrasive or withdrawn or maybe even
doltish, but I knew him to be astonishingly candid and

utterly self-sufficient. I think the only other people who loved him the way I did were probably his patients at the clinic. They held a memorial service for him after a crazy old man, dying of cancer and consumed by an imaginary ten-year-old grudge, had murdered Buddy and then put the gun to his own head. Of course it really wasn't that simple.

And I suppose Yollo loved Buddy too, though love was not a state of being I would normally associate with Yollo. Yollo's story was obscure, even Buddy never knew all of it. He had been a foundling who grew up in juvenile homes and later in juvenile facilities. The name Yollo was given to him because when he had been abandoned on the steps of the home somewhere in the Southwest, I couldn't remember precisely where, he made only one sound: "Yo low, Yo low." The name Current he had picked up later because he was an electrical wizard. He had come to Buddy's clinic when he was about fifteen or sixteen years old and Buddy was astonished to see, looking at his records, that he had no parents and no address to speak of. Before long Buddy's isolated house at the end of a cul-de-sac in a neighborhood called Dogpatch, where the Hell's Angels also had their headquarters, became Yollo's home too, more or less. It turned out Yollo was a flutist of really extraordinary aptitude considering he was entirely self-taught, and he and Buddy would sometimes spend whole evenings playing together, Buddy bent over his grand piano, his long, pliant, strong, and graceful healer's fingers, splattered with freckles and reddish hair, drawing sounds from the instrument of such sadness and joy that even such a philistine as I, who had never attended a symphony in his life, found the greatest peace I had ever known sitting in the shadowy room lit only by a single lamp and listening to this unlikely duet of a doctor who palled with the Hell's Angels and a fat and almost sinister boy with no true name of his own.

I didn't much like Yollo, and certainly didn't trust him although he had never given me any specific reason not to, but in the year and more since Buddy had died we had stayed in touch, maybe because being in each other's presence brought Buddy back.

Yollo was even more high strung and suspicious than usual this morning. "How's tricks?" I asked him.

"Ha ha. Very amusing."

I could afford to be patient. It was a day off. I unbuttoned the top button of my shirt and scratched my crown, two nervous habits of my own. The waiter brought our cappuccinos along with little paper napkins and tiny spoons. "The food will be just a few minutes," he said.

The gas company was doing some work on Broadway in front of the cafe, and men in orange plastic hard hats climbed into and out of the city's bowels through an open manhole. The morning fog had been burned off by a bright California sun. I squinted into it and saw the pie-wedge-shaped Bank of America on the far side of the street. Damn, Lottie's money. I had meant to deposit it on my way to Enrico's so there would be enough in the account to write her a check. She was a shrink and would doubtless call my forgetfulness "avoidance," but she wouldn't relate to it very supportively.

When Yollo picked up his hot cappuccino in both his hands and blew on it, the white foam dusted with chocolate sloshed against the far end of his cup like debris-dirtied surf lapping at Ocean Beach. He had short fingers that were pudgy as far as the first joint and disproportionately slim near the top. They were strikingly graceless fingers with minuscule nails and chalk white cuticles, but they were good fingers for tight, close electrical work, fingers that knew a thing or two about safes and locks as well.

"I had a most interesting evening," he said at last. "I had to make a rather large delivery and found somebody quite unable to take possession of the goods."

"Why was that?"

"Uh, well, to put it as succinctly as possible, he was dead."

"It was a good night for being dead, wasn't it? Harry Shugart. Your buyer."

"Erstwhile buyer," Yollo corrected me. "And it's of the late and lamented Harry Shugart that I speak."

A gas company jackhammer exploded into noisy activity, startling us both. Yollo swept his sharp eyes around the patio and moved his feet tighter together, embracing his satchel.

"How much?" I asked him. It really didn't surprise me that Yollo's business with me this morning concerned Harry Shugart, it just confirmed the tug I had felt reading about his murder. Once a story had its hooks into me it just kept coming at me from all sorts of unexpected angles. But I thought I had put a thirty, a *finis*, to this kind of thing once and for all after being cut adrift by *The Courier*.

"Quite a bit."

"Yeah, but how much?"

"A quarter of a pound of cocaine was involved," he said reluctantly.

"Coke? Since when are you handling coke? That's a dangerous world, cocaine."

He shrugged his shoulders, which were naked except for the straps of the chartreuse jumpsuit, blubberous hairy shoulders. His nonchalance was affected, though. The skin at the corners of his mouth was pale as a fish belly, as if he had been sucking in all night. "I was approached with a very attractive offer; I thought . . ."

"That you'd get rich quick and buy a yacht and sail off to some islands where you could sip rum and tune in baseball games on your shortwave while brownskinned . . . shit." I went to unbutton my top button and found I had already done it.

"Are you *angry*, Benjamin?"

I suppose I was, angry for Buddy, who wouldn't have been angry at all, just sad and concerned and maybe even a bit amused by the prospect of watching Yollo extricate himself from another jam. "Was Harry Shugart's a regular stop? Did he buy grass from you?"

"No, never before." He put his coffee cup back onto the saucer and a second later picked it up again.

"Was this strictly your own deal or were you a courier?"

"I was delivering for some new people in town who are building a network of their own, but the obligation is mine entirely. D'you see?"

"Yeah. Tell me the bad news." The prospect of maybe having to lend him a couple of grand, which was pretty much my entire worth, did not fill me with delight.

"Is $90,000 bad enough to suit you?" He didn't look at me when he said it because he didn't want me to see how frightened he was.

"So many zeroes. So many zeroes spell bad trouble." I had meant to say *add up to*, not *spell*. Mixed metaphors annoy me the way the inconvenient guilt of a client bothers a criminal lawyer.

"Surprise me," Yollo said.

I decided I would. "I was by Shugart's house last night myself. My trip was a no-go too." He didn't register any reaction; he was in too deep to care about pointless coincidences. So I did what I had been trained to do as a reporter, what had become second nature even in remission. I asked him to tell me more about his problems.

"How much is this costing you?" I didn't expect that he had $90,000 of his own, or that he could borrow it from Bank of America. Once you had your drug profits in hand the banks would be glad to launder them for you, but they weren't yet financing busted drug deals—or at least not that I knew.

"The seller won't buy back. The vig is a grand a day. Everybody's got the fooch, nobody is at home to me."

"Yollo, why are you telling *me* about this?" It had been on my mind to ask that question for quite a few minutes.

"Who should I go to?" he asked, turning his palms up. "The city's finest?"

"That doesn't answer my question."

"I need help, Benjamin," Yollo said. It was the first time I had ever heard him say anything that wasn't mocking, cynical, scatological, or about food. For the first time, too, excepting those moments when he was playing his flute with Buddy, he didn't seem prickly and defensive.

All of a sudden he was somebody who could be crushed, soft, a tomato. His nose was sunburned and peeling.

Deep down I had understood all along. He was asking me to fill in for Buddy. Yollo had done me some favors, had even helped me once listen to some people who hadn't wanted to be overheard, but I owed him no binding obligations. "Sleuth," he had called me on the telephone this morning, reminding me of our mutual ties. No wonder he had been able to survive on his own from the age of two years. I spoke to him more gently than I ever had before. "What do you want?"

I could see his relief. "I've been set up, Benjamin. I want to know who did it, who murdered Shugart, and who set me up."

"That may be expecting a bit more than I can do, Yollo."

"Nobody in this town can worm information out of our uniformed civil servants," he said with scornful emphasis, finding his confidence again, "the way you can, dear boy. You *can* find out if my name is coming up downtown, can't you? They're going to set me up, it looked like a setup. I had instructions to come to the side door and when I arrived—I was a bit tardy—the door was ajar. I went inside and found Shugart dead. He was still warm. So I merely wiped my prints off the knob and reversed direction. I'm a made-in-Hollywood villain for this dastardly deed, don't you agree?"

He was right about that, of course. In fact, he was right about quite a few things, not the least of which was that I would welcome the opportunity to show them all what it meant to be a reporter. I felt the tug again, harder, decisive. This was what I knew how to do best, and if I couldn't do it for Thiesmann's fishwrap then I'd do it on my own.

"Okay," I said. "I'll poke around a bit. But it won't be easy, I don't know what kind of welcome I'll get now that I'm not with *The Courier* anymore. It might be like trying to fly without wings."

"Welcome to the aviary," Yollo said.

4

There was a stone coat of arms, something vaguely heraldic, above the door to the bank. It should have been a wood barrel, the one old P. A. Fraccini had slapped his cash down on after the earthquake. The other bankers found their money was too hot to handle: it took three weeks for their vaults to cool down after the fire. But P. A. had loaded his cash in vegetable wagons the moment the earth stopped rocking, and was the first to offer rebuilding loans, setting up shop on barrelheads. His act of precautionary greed was real genius, enriching himself, his customers, and the language.

Inside, a sluggish conga line of impatient customers zigged and zagged between crimson cord barriers. I joined the line to deposit the money for Lottie's alimony. Only two tellers were working, although there were six cages. While I waited I studied the bank's motto on posters tacked to the walls: Service You Can Count On. I counted, and counted, until one of the two tellers closed her window and walked away. Nobody came to take her place.

The branch manager was at his desk at the foot of a spiral catwalk leading to a balcony, chatting on the phone. I walked over and waited for him to acknowledge me. It took quite a while for him to cup his hand over the mouthpiece and look up. Impatiently he said, "Yes?" I reached over and removed the phone from his grip. The handle was clammy. I hung it up. He half rose from his chair, sputtering. When he reached his full height, so that his eyeglasses were level with my chin, he lost a bit of his conviction.

"Just what do you think you're doing?" He was gasping.

Loud enough so that I could be heard by everybody in the hushed bank—I understand why churches are hushed, and libraries, and funeral parlors, but why banks?—I said, "Why don't you go wait on your customers?"

His eyes swung frantically past me looking for help, but the aged guard was studiously looking elsewhere, trying to hide a smile behind a stern appraisal of the housewives and pensioners on line, sizing them up to see if there was a potential bank robber among them. The manager's Adam's apple bobbed. "Just, just, who do you, I mean, what . . ."

"Another word out of your lousy little usurious mouth and I'll carry you over there. You've got one teller waiting on two dozen customers. How about some of that service we can count on?"

"It's the lunch hour," he began, but when I made a short, menacing motion he left his desk and began to snap orders at clerks to open another window. I turned and walked out as an old woman with a shopping bag called after me, "Attaway, big boy."

Waiting for the light to change on the dazzlingly bright street corner, I slipped on my sunglasses. By the time I had a green light, though, I felt like a roughneck, a nice old San Francisco word owing its origins to the high necked sweaters Irish tough guys had once worn. I was rampaging around, tossing drunks on the sidewalk, intimidating upwardly mobile managers, acting as if I were immune from consequences. Cowardly acts. When all my years of hurting Lottie without ever meaning to had at last proved insupportable and I had finally left, I had for a spell felt like a man hanging from a parachute floating down to earth from some great height. It was a weightless, thrilling descent, which I foolishly thought of as freedom.

Then Buddy died and Thiesmann cut me loose from *The Courier* and I hit the earth, hard. By the time I got back on my feet, still badly bruised, I knew that I had lost all the points on the compass by which I had previously located myself in an uncharitable universe. No longer was I Lottie's husband for better or worse, Buddy's friend, or a reporter for *The Courier.* I was somebody named Ben Henry who was no longer young, who had passed that age at which somebody can truly be said to have potential, and I didn't know the first thing about what I wanted now. I still had my sense of right and wrong, but that was as often a torment as a comfort. If I had any toehold at all on this spinning planet it was somehow embedded in the notion that the rent was always due, 365 days a year.

One day something I read would convince me that making a plan and establishing goals was my only chance of salvation, and the next day something I overheard would convince me just as emphatically that only fools made plans. What was most worrisome was that it seemed I didn't really care very much what happened to me. I was daring the Fates to do their worst, a recklessness I shuddered at in my calmer moments. It was excruciatingly embarrassing to be asking who I was at my age; under the circumstances, it was also painful not to know what I wanted. Love, I thought bleakly. By the time I reached the far curb I was grateful for Yollo's misfortunes, which had put me back into harness poking my nose into other people's business.

My car was parked halfway up a curb on a red zone in the alley that ran between Iteli's bookstore, a saloon, and the side wall of a Chinese butcher shop. This was my private spot, but the city had decided it should charge me ten bucks a night to park there. Every morning some meter maid left a reminder of the fee under the windshield, and I had accumulated enough of these tickets to make myself a considerable scofflaw. If the city in its wisdom enacted ordinances that refused to allow a man to park his car off the street and directly behind his own house, then I was quite ready to go on scoffing at their laws.

I hopped onto the freeway and drove lickety-split over to the Hall of Justice. The gray, protective heaviness of the Hall makes it look like an underground kingdom unexpectedly exposed to the harsh light of a California summer afternoon. At the back of the building is the office of the Chief Medical Examiner and Coroner for the City and County of San Francisco, J. Frederic Klein, M.D., practitioner of the morbid sciences.

Dr. Klein, the woman behind the counter told me, would see me in a few minutes. Would I have a seat? I wouldn't, thank you. I leaned my elbows on the counter and watched the clerks and deputy coroners at work at their desks, their tasks appearing no more decisive, no less ordinary, than similar work going on in tens of thousands of government offices and yet, of course, these routine tasks—a man on the telephone, a woman typing in the blanks on a form, even the Chinese guy moving things around on his desk trying to appear as if he had something to keep him occupied—were conclusive because this achingly ordinary room with its metal desks and linoleum covered floor was the dominion of death. The last time I could remember being here was after Boris Mayevsky had done in Buddy and I had made myself come down to read the autopsy report because I was horrified by my own self-control, by the anguish I knew was there but could not feel. I glanced along the counter toward where they kept the workups volume, a heavy, oversize blue loose-leaf ledger. I moved over to it and opened it to the last page. Doctor Fred had already performed his autopsy on the late Shugart, Harry Cornelius.

The body is that of a well-developed, well-nourished 62-year-old white male weighing approximately 170 pounds and measuring approximately 70 inches in length.

Shugart had been wearing slippers, socks, slacks, and a jacket when somebody bound him with a lamp cord, worked him over pretty thoroughly to judge from the contusions and lacerations found on his head, bashed him a good one over the back of the skull with a heavy object, and finished off the job with a single gunshot from close range. The bullet, said the autopsy workup, had "entered the left supra-auricular area of the head, three centimeters above the left earlobe."

"What do you want here?" I looked up and there was the good doctor himself, scratching his left forearm.

"You've sure got a fun prose style."

"I shouldn't be talking with you. Frankly, being seen with you is stupid."

"Then why don't we slip into your office where they won't see us?" I smiled my Burt Lancaster smile, the one with a lot of teeth.

He shook his head but buzzed me through a locked door at the far end of the counter, and I followed him back to his office. It was a large, square room at ground level with skulls and large bones used as bookends holding up sheaths of reports and medical texts. He immediately went to work with a little finger digging at an itch inside his ear. He removed the ticklish particle, inspected it, and then brushed it off against his smock. Doctor Fred, whose job it was to poke and cut the enduringly still, was himself kinetic, forever pulling or scratching some part of himself. His long face had a worried cast; it was the face of a thorough, cautious man. Yet he was daring in his own way, professionally daring. For instance, he had once declared a shooting, in which a cop had killed a drunk who had pointed an empty gun at him and swore he was going to bag himself a cop, to be a suicide, thus creating an entirely new pathological form—the state-of-mind autopsy. He was very good at his job, and dedicated, so every homicide detective in town knew they could rouse him out of bed uncomplaining at four in the morning, especially, they added with a wink, if the murder had the markings of sadomasochism.

"I don't have all day," he said.

"Just one or two questions. Tell me about Shugart."

He stood up. "Go away."

"It doesn't sound like a professional job. I mean, beating him up like that and then bashing him. Maybe they panicked and shot him because they were afraid he'd recover and identify them. Or maybe it was just somebody very angry who got carried away."

"No comment." At least he sat back down. He linked his fingers horizontally just above the desk top. He was thinking about my surmises.

"Look, Doc, I'm not a reporter anymore. I'm not going to print what we talk about."

"A cause for celebration, that is." The thing about Doctor Fred was that he loved his work too much not to talk about it if you gave him half a chance. "Have you considered," he asked me, "whether it might not be consistent with the autopsy results for somebody to have been trying to get him to tell them something and finally becoming exasperated?"

"Hunh. The gunshot killed him? Or was he already dead?"

The professional witness with experience at countless trials was slowly taking over. "That kind of gunshot wound is associated with the collapse of the brain and instantaneous death."

"Did the victim struggle?" My best prosecutorial style.

"There were no disruptions noted that would be consistent with a struggle."

"That suggests he knew them, then?"

"Or was taken by surprise and overpowered. Or decided to submit; perhaps he saw the weapon and decided cooperation was his best course."

"But if that's the case then it's not very likely he was holding out information on them, is it?"

"My charge as coroner is merely to present plausible causes, circumstances, and means of death. In fact, the coroner is the only person charged with that responsibility in the law. It is not to concoct lurid scenarios based on completely insufficient evidence. I leave that entirely to you and your colleagues."

"What did they conk him with?"

He went to work picking out the dirt from beneath a fingernail. I wondered if the little pieces of matter he was removing were the remains of lunch or of Harry Shugart. "Ask upstairs," he said. "Ask your good friends upstairs." He almost smiled.

"Who's handling it?"

"Pressix," Doctor Fred said.

"Okay. Thanks." I stood up and started toward the door when one last question occurred to me. "By the way," I said, feeling like Columbo, even though my question was just an afterthought: "Who claimed the body?"

"It's in the book, look it up."

I shrugged and turned to go again.

"The daughter. She's a bombshell."

"Why, you sly fox. I didn't know you ever noticed living bodies."

As I departed he said, "I've never spoken to you. Anything you attribute to me I'll deny." I waved without looking back—a pathologist almost always has the last word.

Columbo had commercials to convey him from one scene to the next, but I had to take the elevator. There was a palpable wariness as the crowded elevator rose slowly one floor at a time through the dense layers of justice. The Hall was in fact a dangerous place. In the year after they installed a metal detector—buying it secondhand from the airport police—it had beeped for knives, ice picks, containers of chemical Mace, rounds of live ammunition, fireworks, hypodermic needles, bludgeons, brass knuckles, kung fu instruments, imitation pistols, a gas-pellet gun, and a loaded .38 revolver. I had written a story about it for *The Courier*. There had been fourteen muggings, two rapes, twenty-seven robberies, and a murderous assault on a transvestite in a men's room. I had thought my story was kind of ironic, maybe I'd taken too many literature courses in college. The constabulary certainly hadn't seen the humor in it.

Just as I reached for the knob of the door with HOMICIDE stenciled on its frosted glass window, it opened from within and there appeared a young blonde woman with perfect skin and dark glasses. She had the kind of looks that make cab drivers readjust their rearview mirrors. Behind her, his massive brown fist engulfing the doorknob, his diamond pinky ring gleaming, was Inspector Franklin Delano Roosevelt Pressix. I stepped aside to let her pass and said to Pressix, "Just the man I was looking for."

Pressix is one of the few men I've ever met who make me feel insignificantly small. I'm about six three myself but Pressix was several inches taller. He had a face full of small bumps and deeply worn furrows like a topographical photograph of a cold and uninhabitable planet, a huge nose, and a head that seemed almost too heavy to hold up.

"We'll be in touch," he said to the girl, who nodded and walked toward the elevators. She had long legs and a supple stride. We both watched her.

"Caught anything juicy?" I asked him.

"What you want here?" Everybody around the Hall was certainly glad to see me again.

"The daughter a suspect?" I asked, nodding in the direction the girl had gone. Maybe I could make him think I knew something.

Pressix was wearing a shirt in a shade of pale orange that was loose around his thick neck, the pants of a herringbone suit, an amber tie with a diamond stickpin, and a standard issue police revolver in a holster under his arm. He ignored my question.

"Who you represent, Sonny?"

"Four generations of Henrys, Inspector. The masses, thirsting for knowledge. The spirit of the curious. And I guess you could say one client with whom I haven't discussed a fee."

"What you mean, a client?"

"Somebody with an interest in a homicide."

"You carrying a license to snoop?"

"Maybe we can exchange information. You got a suspect?"

He grunted and went back toward the bullpen where the homicide detectives had their desks. I tagged along. Some of the desks were cluttered and others were orderly or almost empty, but every one of them had one thing in common, a framed photograph of the wife and kids, or, if they were divorced as a lot of them were, just one of the kids. Pressix's wife was a stately lightskinned woman and his children were teenagers, a boy and two girls. One of the girls was wearing a graduation robe and holding a rolled diploma. Pressix sat down in a swivel chair that could barely contain him. I sat in a folding chair beside his desk.

A young detective I hadn't seen before came over and stood there, wanting apparently to tell Pressix something but not willing to talk until he got an indication of whether I was okay or not. He had a round Irish face and a shock of black hair that was neatly trimmed around his ears but fell over his forehead despite what I guessed were frequent attempts to comb it back in place. His arms were very long and hung from broad shoulders almost as low as his knees. He held himself like an athlete.

"Yeah?" Pressix asked him.

That was the signal the new boy needed. "The coroner says there was semen traces. You were right." His voice was high pitched.

Pressix grunted.

"You figured that from the scissors in the boot?" There was admiration in the young detective's question.

"Somethin' they do," Pressix answered. "Hung himself in the closet to jerk off while he was holdin' the scissors to cut himself down befoah he passes out or he comes, whichever is first. Looked like a suicide but it was this othuh thing."

"Some guy hung himself by the neck to jerk off?" I said.

"Don't go knockin' it till you try it," Pressix said. "Okay," he told the young detective, dismissing him. I had known a lot of juvenile cops, in fact most of them had their development arrested in a high-school locker room, but I had never known one who was green in spirit. Even a kid like the young detective for all his furry-tailed enthusiasm had eyes that were already shut down.

"Now you, Sonny."

"That your new partner? What happened to Cannibal?"
Cannibal Figone, Pressix's longtime partner, had acquired
his nickname before he came over to Homicide, when he
was still in Vice. One night during a drug raid he had
found a jar of grayish powder that he had never seen before. Figone smelled it, nothing. He tasted it, nothing. So
he said to the woman whose place he was raiding, "You're
gonna have to help me, sister. What is this stuff?"

"My Uncle Harry's ashes," replied the lady. "You bastard."

"Cannibal pass the lieutenant's exam, he's over Taraval
Station," Pressix said.

"Who's the new guy?"

"Flynn. He be all right if he don't stop to cross himself
before he chase a cronk into a church. He don't work out,
you get him a job hacking, huh?" His big chest heaved
twice. A laugh, I presumed.

"You know what I'm wondering," I said, not acknowl-
edging that his barb had caused a twinge in my gut. "I'm
wondering how come you pull all the easy ones? Take
Shugart. No pressure from upstairs, no toes to be avoided.
Your kind of case, a piece of cake."

Pressix leaned back and his chair groaned in dismay.
"I know how to keep my mouth shut. You go ahead, quote
me on that, Sonny."

"I'm not in that line of work anymore. But listen, was
anything taken from Shugart's house?"

Pressix gave me a sharp look.

"I heard that what they conked him with is missing."

"You gonna print that? That's something I don' want
them to know we know."

"About the only place I could print anything in this
town is on a men's room wall. No, I'm not gonna print
anything."

"Was a jade bookend," Pressix said.

"No indication of robbery as a motive?"

He shook his head. "Not so far, we're still lookin'."

"Forcible entry?"

"Unh unh."

"Suspects?"

"You know I can't talk about that, Sonny. Liberals like you jump all over me I go talkin' 'bout suspects."

I fumbled in my pocket for a cigarette. Briefly I considered telling him what Yollo had told me and instantly decided that as well as being a breach of confidentiality, it never was wise to offer more information than you had to. I tried to keep what I was thinking off my face, but Pressix was too good a cop to miss it entirely.

"You know somethin' you want to tell me, Sonny?" His face, more gray than brown, remained impassive as melted chocolate.

"I've always wondered how a big, uncomplicated guy like you got named after a cripple who could outscheme Stalin. It's just a hunch, you know, but have you checked out a drug angle?"

His eyelids drooped. "Ah'm waitin'," he said softly.

"Hell, Franklin, don't wait. Go out there in the mean streets of our city and earn that munificent municipal salary. Track down the bad guys without fear or favor."

"You know somethin' or you jus' fiddlin' youh fandango?"

"Check it out, Inspector. Then maybe you can tell me."

5

My passenger held a compact and watched herself dab on eyeshadow with a tiny brush. The number of women who applied their makeup in the back seat of my cab was exceeded only by the number of men who asked me, "Know where I can find some girls?"

When she paid me and got out I was around the corner from Leo's and ready for a break. It was a good night; the city had a steady flow to it that I had caught early and held onto, never pushing too hard but just letting the current of business carry me along. Some nights had a furious energy that required a heavy foot and a quick eye merely to keep up; others were calm and dull as a shallow lake on a windless evening, and that's when strategy and instinct were more valuable than driving skill, but the best nights were the ones like tonight where you never rode empty for long but you never had to push toward the limits of your skill or knowledge of the deep unmistakable pulse of the town. On such a night it was natural that just when I felt ready for a break I would find myself outside Leo's, which was one of my spots, a place with all the amenities and attitudes I needed to conduct a successful and efficient break: fast, accurate service, inexpensive food to go, no lines or delays, a clean bathroom, and a pay phone. In fact, Leo's lacked a phone, but there was a public booth just up the block on Bush Street.

34

It was warm and bright and good smells rose off the steam table. The room was L-shaped and painted yellow. There were varnished pine tables. The big clock on the back wall, which had bagels where the numbers should have been, showed the time to be about half past nine bagels. Leo was where he was seven nights a week, 365 nights a year except for the Jewish high holy days, at the end of the long counter past the hot dogs and hot plate specials, beyond the sandwich meats and salads and chopped liver, past the cakes and strudels and Danish arrayed under glass, on his feet at his cash register looking exhausted.

"Leo, you need a vacation, you work too hard." What I always said first.

He smiled a smile as robust as the soup they serve in the city jail. I might as well have told Sisyphus that Club Med was running a Greek Isles special. Leo was a paunchy, gray-faced seventy-year-old, a living testimony to the effects of tired blood and collapsed arches, a man who swore by Dr. Scholl.

"So how's by you?"

"Nothing to complain about. You want to give me a cheese Danish and a cup for coffee?" You drew the coffee from an electric urn back beneath the bagel clock. There were a couple of better known and far more expensive Jewish delis further downtown across from the legitimate theaters, but only Leo's with its bottomless ennui and its superior chopped liver and thick salami sandwiches reminded me even a little of the places in Chicago where I had learned the true meaning of corned beef on rye. Leo's corned beef wasn't much, but he could hardly be blamed for that, isolated as he was in San Francisco among herds of pugnacious Irishmen who thought a good time was getting drunk and pounding each other senseless and whose approach to corned beef was to—forgive them, Father, for they know not—boil it with cabbage.

When I offered to pay he waved my money away. He hadn't let me pay for anything since I had written a story a few years back celebrating his joint and telling how the landlord was trying to turn him out after thirty years because a savings and loan was willing to pay triple Leo's rent. The S&L was very persuasive. They had explained to Leo how even an Episcopalian church had reached a compromise with them, moving the house of worship to the second floor and installing a small shopping arcade including their branch office, and a parking garage, at ground level. When that didn't cut the mustard with Leo, so to speak, their next move had been to offer incentives in the form of cushy early retirement, since Leo had an airtight lease with another five years to run. This showed a basic lack of comprehension on the part of the S&L, as they were dealing with a man who hadn't raised his prices since Lyndon Johnson was in the White House and who had been working twelve-hour days since before the S&L's senior vice president was in diapers. Nonetheless Leo was plenty frightened by the move they were putting on him because he knew the sum total of his landlord's scruples came to the shape of one of his bagels. Evidently Leo thought my story had helped to chase the S&L back under its rock, and ever since he hadn't charged me, which meant I couldn't go in there as much as I would have liked without becoming a schnorrer.

"There's somebody wants to meet you," Leo said.

"I got to get back to work, Leo." For all that the night had been nice and easy that didn't mean I could afford to sit down and shmooze. I was in a taxi frame of mind, which might be described as the sensation of information spinning in time to the tires, that information consisting of my route, my destination, traffic patterns, clogged intersections to avoid on later trips, the time of day and its implications for traffic flow, the dispatch radio, conversations with passengers, tentative plans on which way to head next after I dropped, whether I was on pace for a $20 hour, what my net take would be if I continued averaging $20 an hour until the end of the shift, whether anybody on the sidewalk was flagging a cab, the time of day again (this time to help to decide where in the city business might be best—and the day of the week for the same reason), and, of course, the approximate distance to Leo's and a couple of other places where I could spin in and spin out the door again and back to the taxi without any excessive loss of momentum. "Maybe some other time."

"A minute it'll take while you eat your Danish. What? Your time is so valuable, Mr. Taxi Driver?" He didn't wait for an answer, just came out from behind the register and started toward a table where an elderly couple was looking expectantly toward us. There were always some older German and East European Jews dawdling over coffee in Leo's place, which was seldom true of the theater district delis and one more reason why Leo's felt like home. I was only half Jewish myself, but my peripheral connection to Leo's place did revive certain memories of my father that I found less troubling or painful than most of the others. The doctors had said his heart failed and I accepted that, though I didn't think Dr. Cooperman and I had understood the meaning of the phrase in all the same ways.

The meter that was my mind on nights behind the wheel made me abrupt. "I'm sorry, Leo, can't tonight." It made me feel lousy to disappoint him, so I smiled at the old couple on my way out. One more reason to wonder why I always was the thief.

Back in my taxi I sat with the motor running for a moment listening to Doris on the dispatch radio and deciding whether to head downtown or circle the block and make a pass at Polk Street, but before I had made up my mind a couple of guys in nearly matching outfits—tight jeans and black leather vests over their tank tops—came over.

"Are you available?" one of them asked.

One or both of them was wearing a strong scent, more herbal than sweet. It overpowered the distinctive smell of the interior of the cab, which mingled memories of thousands of human body odors with the newish plastic smell of the seats and dashboard already coated with grime that would never wash away. But I soon stopped noticing the scent and in fact forgot all about my passengers until I glanced in the rearview mirror a few blocks along and was startled to see them there. You could completely forget that there was a load in the back seat, or where you were taking them. Sometimes I rode for blocks without being able to remember what my destination was, or whether I was heading the right way. Somehow you always remembered in time, though.

"He's got a new car," one was saying to the other. "A red convertible. Really flash."

"How overstated."

"Well, *you* know Ricky. He's always been tacky," the first one said coyly, backing away from his admiration for the red ragtop. "What else would you expect?"

"He is *just* a bit much," said the one whose opinions seemed to matter more, the Top Dog.

"And that impossible queen he lives with."

"Ooh, she's too good for him," said the Top Dog. They both laughed. I glanced in the rearview and saw that the Bottom Dog was nuzzling the other fellow's neck and quickly averted my eyes. So much happened in the back seat. People had sex there, and others, out on a date, had nothing at all to say to each other. Cocaine had been snorted and passengers had moaned with pain, but not the man who had staggered in bleeding from a stab wound in his chest that he said his wife had inflicted on him; he remained perfectly quiet trying to staunch the flow of blood with both his hands and refused to be taken to the hospital. There were pissers and pukers and people who just outright smelled bad. I didn't have to be driving a taxi, I told myself for the ten-thousandth time, I could pick up and go elsewhere and catch on with another paper. The thought of tucking in my tail and leaving San Francisco filled me with bitterness. It had become my town, I had made it mine, and the truth of the matter was I was delighted by the private knowledge that not too many hours after I finished in the taxi I would be in a different world altogether, back at work on the Shugart murder. The daughter seemed like the next logical step. I wanted to talk to her and get a look around Shugart's house, if I could.

The Bottom Dog was saying something about his haircut.

"It's so floppy," said the Top Dog.

"Incredibly easy to handle, really."

"Well, he does divine work," said the Top Dog. "But I never get my hair done by old lovers."

"Oh, I know, he's so hard to get an appointment with. Sometimes I really have to wonder just who he thinks he is."

"Daddy's little man, that's who."

"Oh God, wasn't it *horrible*? I mean, I hear he absolutely went to pieces."

"Well, his father found out. That's what I heard."

"Did Ricky tell you that?"

"I don't need Ricky to tell me anything. I heard that his father told Ricky he was going to teach that nasty old man a lesson."

"Oh, come on."

"You don't believe me? A lesson."

"Isn't murdering him a bit much?"

"Well, *I* wouldn't be surprised."

Could they possibly be talking about Ricky Thiesmann? It had been around for a long time that the son of *The Courier*'s publisher was gay, and while on the one hand that was something which in some quarters of San Francisco didn't raise eyebrows, it was also still the kind of thing that was only whispered about in other quarters. Attitudes changed and didn't change at the same time. Could the Top Dog possibly be right, could Thiesmann possibly have killed Shugart? There was the tug again: *my* story. But this one tugged deeper and more painfully, a harpoon in my gut which, resist as I might, sucked me down into my hatred for Thiesmann and everything he represented; scalding, jumbled memories.

Mazer had called me into his managing editor's cubicle and closed the door behind me, something he hadn't ever done before. Without any preliminaries he told me I was fired. They would give me two months' severance pay, but they wanted me out of the building by the end of the day. At first I had acted like it must be a joke even though I knew it wasn't. Mazer was a phlegmatic German as likely to participate in a practical joke as Nancy Reagan was to spit watermelon seeds at a state dinner.

"You're kidding," I said. My heart was pounding. "How can you fire me when I'm this close to really getting the good stuff about the police department nailed down? It's taken a whole year to get this stuff."

Mazer wore a hearing aid and when it suited him he paused an extra beat or two before he answered. "That's the trouble," Mazer finally said. "I showed Mr. Thiesmann the memo you sent me. He doesn't want any more police exposés. He doesn't want you." Mazer looked out the window toward the Old Mint and then back at me. "He says you're a disgrace to the profession." I could hear the quotation marks of the careful journalist around what he was saying. "He says you're biased, reckless, very careless about stretching facts to suit your preconceptions, and not up to the standards of *The Courier*."

I was breathing hard. These were things I had heard before, more than once, but I had always shrugged them off. I had my standards, I didn't need theirs. "Oh, is that all?"

"No. Mr. Thiesmann said *The Courier* was no longer going to be responsible for cleaning up the messes you make."

"And what did you say, Mazer?"

He didn't reply but he clenched his jaw and his mouth curled angrily.

"This stuff about the cops and drug money is the first hard investigative piece the paper's had since the assessor story."

"Ben," Mazer said, touching his hearing aid with his fingertips, "your assessor story cost us fifty thousand dollars to settle out of court. And this stuff about the cops and drugs is even worse; you don't really have it nailed down, and if you weren't such a goddamn hothead you could see that."

"I can't help it if your lawyer is chickenshit. Tell Thiesmann to get a lawyer who knows his business and to drop that blockhead who rowed with him at Stanford."

"*The Courier* doesn't want to be going to court every time you get a bug up your ass. I get the feeling lately that you're out of control. Don't you understand that you're being reckless with *his* reputation?"

I kept arguing, knowing it was pointless but not wanting to face the end of the conversation. "A bug up my ass? That's what you call it when there's upper echelon cops living beyond their means and palling around at Lake Tahoe with the pinky-ring crowd? What the hell is wrong with this paper? Your idea of an investigation is to send your wimpy food critic to the ballpark to tell us the hot dogs ain't pure beef."

Mazer shrugged. I looked past him out into the city room where here and there reporters were working at their video display terminals, or talking into the mouthpieces that clipped onto their heads, or reading the last edition of the paper, which had just come up. Nobody seemed to be paying any particular attention to us in Mazer's glass cubicle. Auden was so right about suffering, how it takes place while someone else is eating or opening a window or just walking dully along. Mazer still hadn't replied and when he didn't take up the argument I knew that it was all over. My skin was goosebumps and my heart was racing.

"I want to talk to Thiesmann myself."

"He has nothing to say to you."

"What's that supposed to mean?"

Mazer paused for that disconcerting beat. "Just what it sounds like. He refuses to see you."

I cleared out the same afternoon, but it hadn't been until I woke up before dawn the next morning in the grip of an awful nightmare which I couldn't remember except that it involved my father's disapproval that it truly sunk in that I wasn't a reporter at *The Courier* anymore. I flew to Mexico, to Isla Mujeres, but got tired of the beach pretty soon—too many thoughts percolating in the sun, it was only a few months since Buddy had been killed—so I came back home and hung out in bars and cafes and met a lot of women who I saw just once and then never wanted to see again. My severance pay had run out when I was offered a job at a pretty good salary in a public relations firm, but I knew I couldn't flak. At least my lies were my own. I took a job instead at Checker Cab without mentioning to anybody there that I'd been at *The Courier*; I couldn't see that there was any reason to mention it.

The things Thiesmann had said, speaking through Mazer, never entirely stopped gnawing at me. Someday, I knew, I would make him face me himself.

"Driver, you just went past it."

With a wrench I returned to the taxi. "Oh, Jesus, I'm sorry. Daydreaming."

They paid and left me there thinking murderous thoughts about Richard Cornelius Thiesmann II.

6

She was past me the moment I opened the door. "Where's your fridge?" she said. "I brought a bottle of wine." She held up the bottle for me to see.

"I don't drink white wine. Erica, what are you doing here?" I was still standing at the open door with my hand on the knob.

"I *knew* you wouldn't like white wine. That's why I brought it, because I knew you wouldn't have any." She went over to my Murphy bed, which I hadn't bothered to fold up into its closet, and dropped her shoulder bag on it.

"Listen, I'm busy." I had seen her once, no, twice before. The first time after I was back from Mexico when I seemed to be running a girl-of-the-night contest. The other time I had bumped into her late one night when I was out for a walk and she was coming out of the club where she danced on Broadway and we had gone to her apartment up in Marin. I remembered three things about her. Her name, that she was studying communications at Berkeley, and that I didn't like the way her skin felt. She was very shapely, but slippery. That, and her incessant conversation. She had written to me twice and called a couple of times but I hadn't been sufficiently lonely to touch her again.

"I'm not going to interrupt you," she said. "I haven't

43

had a shower in three days, the damn water rationing, and I smell awful. I only want to borrow your shower.'' She pulled her blouse over her head. She wasn't wearing a bra.

"Erica, for Christ sake.''

"I *need* a shower.'' She went into the bathroom unzipping her skirt and closed the door behind her. It had been a while since I had been with her, and I couldn't remember so much the way her skin felt as the rest of it. I got back in bed, where I had been when she knocked, and resumed reading the paper and sipping my second cup of the morning. I knew how full of empty self-loathing I would feel when we were through, but my libido was staging a palace coup.

Erica came out of the shower with one of my towels wrapped around her hair and another one worn like a skirt and sat down on the edge of my bed. She was damp and pink. I could feel the warmth of the shower on her. "You're the neatest man I ever met,'' she said.

"Why do you say that?''

"First, your towels were folded over the rack. Second, there was no hair in the bathtub; *all* straight men have hair in the bathtub. Third, no toothpaste sticking to the basin. Fourth, you're in bed but you already made it up. Well, listen, thanks for the shower. That was great.'' She didn't make any move to leave. I was still holding the paper in one hand. "Oh, come on,'' she said. "Stop playing the strong and silent type.'' She rolled over next to me, the towel around her hips unknotting and falling beneath her as she did, and rested her head on my shoulder. Her touch was very gentle, surprisingly so for an energetic girl. I didn't like gentle women. I let go of the paper and rubbed the concave flesh inside her hipbone. Slippery. She raised her head and cradled it on a palm with her elbow crooked against my pillow and looked at me appraisingly.

"You know the only things I can read in that paper are Garfield and the horoscopes,'' she said.

"That goes to show you've got very good sense. The horoscopes are the most reliable thing in *The Courier*.''

"It's an awful newspaper. Do you know what my prof at

Berkeley said—oh, and now that Harry Shugart's dead I don't think I want to read *The Bulletin* either. He said . . ."

"Who do you think killed Shugart?"

"How should I know?"

"You want to be a reporter. Aren't you curious?"

"I want to be in communications. That's different."

"Oh."

"I was in his column once."

"Oh, yeah? What for?"

"Well, really it was about my father, something he did. He held a twenty-first-birthday party for me at The Washbag, and, you know, Harry Shugart was there. I really miss him. I don't mean him, I mean I only met him that once and all he said was happy birthday, you know, I mean his column. I read it my whole life, ever since I can remember. *You* probably didn't like it, right?"

"Why do you say that?"

"Because whatever everybody else likes you don't. You want to think of yourself as a rebel but you're just a Peck's Bad Boy."

I stopped stroking her hip and withdrew my hand. "A Peck's Bad Boy? Is that what you think I am?"

She pushed the towel off her hair and with her free hand tossed her hair loose. It was long, thick brown hair. The motion made her breasts rise and fall. They were round and firm breasts; she couldn't have been more than twenty-two. "Uh huh. Like with me. You want to pretend there's nothing special between us, but I know you know there is."

"No, there isn't."

"You see? How many guys do you think would talk to me like that in bed? Do you *know* how many times I'm hit on every day? And you're barely willing to let me in when I show up at your door. So, naturally, you're the one I want." She wasn't able to achieve the tragic effect she wanted.

"You think because I didn't call you and didn't answer

your letters and don't act entirely pleased to see you, that shows I'm really crazy about you?''

Her hands were wide and her fingers short. She took very good care of her nails. She reached out and took my hand and put it against one of her breasts, guiding it down from there. When she was satisfied it could be trusted to keep busy without her help she began to unbuckle my belt.

''I'm not crazy about you, Erica.''

''I suppose you'd kick me out of bed.'' She was unzipping my pants.

''Not now,'' I admitted. ''But afterward.''

She didn't believe me again. ''Oh, right.'' She was sitting up pulling my pants off and then she was running her hands along the insides of my legs.

''How else can I show you how much I care?'' I said to the top of her head as she bent over me.

An hour later I was on my way up those parapet steps again, taking them two at a time but not running. I didn't know what to say to Judy Shugart, how to begin. I could no longer say I was with *The Courier*, which had been my foot in the door in places I wasn't especially welcome before. I leaned on the bell, setting off the chimes. What could I say? ''Madam, your taxi''?

Through the glass door I saw a man approaching. He was slim and lithe and wore a navy blue suit that had been cut and stitched by a tailor whose name ended in *o* or *i*. His face was blunt and angular with sharp planes and his nose was straight but slightly off-center, giving him a lopsided appearance. He had sensual lips and thick black hair. He opened the door.

''Yes?'' he said.

''Miss Shugart, please.'' That was pretty snappy, but it didn't solve my problem.

''She's indisposed. Anything I can do?'' Up close I saw that there was a faint silver pinstripe pattern in the blue of his suit. Up close, too, I sized him up as a tough boy, maybe private security, but somehow I doubted that.

''My business is personal,'' I told him. It was coming home to me how much I had traveled courtesy of Thiesmann and his daily dream machine. *The Courier* had made me somebody. Where did I stand now?

He was looking me over pretty carefully, and I was glad I had decided to wear my poplin suit, my Bally shoes, and a knit tie. They helped give me a feeling of legitimacy. I restrained my hand from wandering to my cheek to check out how much stubble had accumulated since I had last shaved and as I did I remembered Lottie's money and felt a pang of familiar guilt.

"What did you say your name was?"

"I didn't." We already detested each other. I could see it in his too-handsome face, made more striking by the off-center nose, which I would have rather smashed with a baseball bat than talked to. It was his ease I hated most. "It's Henry, Ben Henry. I have some information and a few questions. For her."

"Are you a reporter? Is that it?" He sneered when he said it. His eyes were dark and skittish; they kept roaming over me.

"Listen, why don't you tell her I'm here? I think I can be of some help."

"Forget it. Get lost."

I didn't budge. Our eyes locked. He began to close the door in my face.

"Hey," I said, and instinctively put out my hand to keep the door from shutting. He pushed harder. I resisted. Welcome to the aviary, isn't that what Yollo had said? Just as I thought the thick glass panes might begin to shatter we were both frozen by the sound of high heels clicking across the parquet in our direction. He half turned and I took advantage of his momentary indecision to step forward so that I was standing just inside the door in a main hall. There were two rooms to my right, one with a sliding glass door, and through it I could see formal furnishings: a glass coffee table, leather chairs. The room looked more as if it were for display than for regular use. At the far end of the hall was a room, which, from the little bit of it I could see through an open door, was the sitting room actually in use. There were bookshelves visible filled with books with glossy covers, and I saw the edge of what I thought was a pinball machine. Judy Shugart was approaching along the hall.

"Jerry, what is it?" She had a voice like green apples, clean and tangy. Reluctantly he let his hand fall from where he had been holding it against my chest.

"This creep's a reporter," he said. "He tried to shove his way in and I wasn't allowing it."

"Yes?" She turned her shockingly blue eyes on me. Her eyes were set wide apart and were almond shaped. She had a broad, smooth forehead above which her golden hair was swept up in a tight bun. She wore round black earrings that matched her necklace, a black silk blouse, a white skirt made of some nubby material, and high-heeled pumps. Mourning had never before been so fetching.

"I'm sorry to be disturbing you at a time like this, but I'm here for a friend of yours who has some information regarding your father's murder. He also has a couple of questions I thought maybe you could help answer. Your butler here was attempting to get his arm broken." I smiled only after he flushed with anger. She almost smiled too—a certain narrowing of the eyes and a pull at the corners of her wide mouth glossed in a demure shade of blushing pink—and then caught herself. I was encouraged. "I'm Ben Henry," I told her.

"Who sent you? You said a friend? Somebody I know?"

"It would be better if we could talk alone." I was pretty sure she didn't lack confidence in her ability to handle any man on her own.

"Mr. Cole is my fiancé. He's helping me, uh, handle things. I'm sure that he didn't mean to be rude, it's just . . . well, you understand."

"She asked you a question," Cole said.

"Yollo Current," I said, talking to her. They exchanged an involuntary glance, one I wasn't meant to see.

"We don't know anybody named Yollo Current," Cole said. Judy Shugart laid a hand on his sleeve. The nails were painted a deep red but the fingers had very little character, and that disappointed me. I would find it hard to go in a big way for a woman whose hands were not interesting. Hands tell as much as eyes because they are just as involved in apprehending the world. Unlike all the rest of her, her hands were merely pretty, smooth and straight. "Jerry," she said, "why don't I listen to what Mr. Henry has to say? I'm sure he wants to help. You could make that phone call we talked about." Her black silk blouse had a deep V. There was a pucker at her throat. It palpitated.

He started to object, but she cut him off. "Please," she said. "Please, Jerry."

Cole hesitated, looking from her to me and back again. Her hand was still on his arm. His chest heaved silently. "I'll be in the kitchen if you need me, but I don't like it." He turned to go.

"Help yourself to anything you find in the fridge." I couldn't help myself.

He swung back toward me. "You're going to get your face mashed, sweetheart." His fists were balled and I could see by the automatic way he shuffled his feet one in front of the other that he had spent some time in the ring.

"I'm trembling," I told him.

"Jerry!"

"Shit," he said, but he turned again and went off down the hall and into the door she had come out of.

"That last remark was unnecessary, Henry." The almost-smile was playing hide-and-seek around her eyes and her mouth. It was hard not to want to play with her. She said my name as if it were a private joke.

"I suppose not, but if we only said what was necessary there wouldn't be much to say between good morning and good night."

"What about pass the sugar?"

"Or, which side of the bed do you sleep on?"

She laughed but didn't keep on with it. Her teeth were white and regular, but her canines overlapped the teeth beside them.

I was pretty sure I was being handled, with care. I liked it. Girls like Erica thought that seduction involved what you gave away, but Judy Shugart, who was not much older, had probably always known that it was what you witheld that aroused.

''Let's go in here.'' She slid open the glass door to the formal room to our right and I followed her in. It was a cold room, painted white. The colors in the Danish throw rugs complemented the whites and pale browns and aquas of the furniture. The glass coffee table had stainless steel legs and the standing lamp was also stainless. The framed prints were all European art deco. The room was banal; it seemed to have been done by an interior decorator. On the far wall was a door painted white also, which may have been a closet or may have connected elsewhere. She sat in the corner of a small couch covered in a rich brown velveteen corduroy and indicated that I should take the Danish leather chair at the end of the coffee table closer to her.

Judy Shugart crossed her legs. She took a cigarette out of a black enamel box on the coffee table, so I reached into my pocket and took out one of my own and lit them both. Just as the flame reached her cigarette she looked up into my eyes from an inch or two away and said, ''What does Yollo Current want?''

I laughed and the match went out. I handed the box of matches to her and leaned back in my chair. The leather was buttery and the chair contoured in a way to be remarkably comfortable. ''You do know Yollo, then?''

''No, not really. I've heard his name. The policeman in charge of the investigation, Inspector Pressix, asked me if I'd ever heard of him. I told him no. He, I mean Pressix, said that he was a drug dealer and they were looking for him to question him.''

That was interesting. I was trying to choose what I wanted to say with care. ''Yollo *is* a dealer. According to what I've heard, my information, he was supposed to be making a delivery here the night before last, the night your father was killed. He never did make the delivery. From what Pressix told you it sounds like they regard Yollo as a suspect. Do you find it plausible that your father would have been buying a quarter-pound of cocaine?''

She laughed, a disbelieving laugh. "That's preposterous," she said. "You can't imagine how preposterous. Two glasses of Lafite-Rothschild was Harry's idea of a drug overdose."

"You're certain? He made it sound in the column like he had toasted the coming of many a dawn.''

"Well, maybe a couple of liters, then, but he still talks— I mean, he—he used to talk about how he had smoked what he called a recfer in Hawaii way back during the war and he couldn't understand what all the fuss was about because all it had done to him was make him sleepy. It took quite a bit to make Harry sleepy usually, he was always afraid that if he went to sleep he'd miss something. I'm the same way, Henry.''

She had a way of saying my name that made me feel as if we were conspiring. I would have been content to sit there shooting the breeze about Lafite-Rothschild and Hawaiian reefers with Judy Shugart until the cows came home.

"Oh, listen," she said. "Do you want some coffee or something?''

I wanted a cup of coffee all right, but when I thought about Jerry-baby out there sulking in the kitchen I told her, "No, thanks." I remembered all the times I had slopped some coffee while trying to take notes—I seemed to be drawn only into lines of work that involved spilling coffee on myself—and decided that so far I liked whatever I was doing now better than being a reporter. But every once in a while my hand wanted to fly toward my breast pocket and whip out my pad and pen for fear I'd forget something important.

"Do you have any idea why somebody might have wanted to kill your father?''

"Harry had a lot of enemies, he zinged a lot of people in his column. But would Abagail Goodman want to murder him just because he calls her The Leaning Tower of

Compromise?'' Abagail Goodman was the mayor. Her trademark was a cane.

"Do you trust the police to get to the bottom of this?''

"I never thought about it. Shouldn't I?''

"Myself, I wouldn't trust them with a broken Timex. Where were you when it happened?''

"You ask a lot of questions, you know that? I was out with a girlfriend and then I was supposed to meet Jerry later. My car was acting funny, stalling and stuff. I'm not real mechanical or anything, so I came back here to leave the car and call a cab. Jerry showed up a few minutes later; I was late and he came to see if everything was all right. We went out in his car, we had a drink at Cafe Royale, and when we got back again the police were here.''

"What time were you here?''

She gave me a look. "Are you always this suspicious?''

"Occupational disability.''

"You're not a reporter, are you? Are you a private detective?''

I guffawed, not one of my most attractive gestures. "At the moment what I am seems to be nearly an existential question. Jer-baby wasn't so far wrong, I used to be a reporter at *The Courier* but not anymore.''

"I thought I knew your name. I heard from . . . You were the one who wrote all those stories about the cops. Oh, hey, you just love getting in trouble, don't you? You can be dangerous, can't you, Henry? Honestly, I don't see what I can do to help you, whatever it is you're after. I'm just a scatterbrain, that's what Harry used to say. I've been away at school mostly, so I hardly ever saw Harry.''

"Ah," I said. "And what time was it you said you came back here to drop off your car?''

She laughed and put her hand on the back of mine. I felt as if I'd been burned. "I'm not really sure.'' She withdrew her hand and I breathed an inner sigh of relief and regret. "It might have been eleven, maybe later. I'm not very good about time; I mean I'm usually late. You don't wear a watch either but you're a real punctual kind of guy, aren't you?''

"I'm having quite a day. I've been told I'm neat and punctual. If I could take shorthand I'd make somebody a hell of a secretary.''

"That would depend,'' she said.

"On?''

"On which side of the desk you took shorthand on.''

"Would you pass the sugar, please?''

There was a momentary silence during which I thought she was looking past me toward the glass door and I wondered if Cole was out there, but I didn't turn around. Or maybe she had decided it was time to pull back a bit. I didn't want to believe it was that easily turned on and off. "Which cab company was it you said you called?'' I asked her.

"Luxor. I always call Luxor. They have all those nice gray old men driving for them, wearing ties. Are you certain that Yollo Current was coming here?''

"Yes.''

"I really do like you, you know, you don't have to be so suspicious,'' she said. "You didn't come in here full of phony condolences. I'm sick of condolences. I never much liked Harry, if the truth be known. But I'm sorry for him, dying like that. Does that sound unforgivably cold? The other thing I like about you is you're reckless. And I think you look cute in your little suit and tie. You don't usually wear them, do you? Here,'' she said. She walked to a pad on a teak wall unit where there was a telephone, and scribbled something. "Here's my private number. If you find out anything else, call. Or just call anyway.''

I stood up, dismissed, and took the slip of paper. In her heels she was quite tall. She smelled smashing. We walked to the door side by side.

"See ya,'' she said.

I started down the steps, amused by how easily she had handled me and how much I had enjoyed it. I had learned quite a bit, too. She was not exactly trustworthy, had a thug for a fiancé, and lied even when it didn't matter. I hadn't been as drawn to a woman in as long as I could remember.

I had also accomplished the simplest of the tasks Yollo had set me. Pressix did regard him as a suspect. Somebody had dropped a dime on him the same night Shugart died. How had Pressix known so fast about Yollo's being there?

What I loved best about questions was how the good ones begat more questions. I put my hand in my pocket and touched the paper with her number on it.

7

It was nearly one in the morning when Aretha showed up in a black designer evening suit, a snakeskin jacket draped over her bare shoulders. I waved her over. She waved back and started toward me, looking incongruous among the horseplayers and wise guys who hung at the all-night coffee shop. I leaned down and pecked at the lips she stood on her tippytoes to offer.

The moment we sat down Frances slammed two coffee cups in front of us, pouring mine first, then filling Aretha's until it ran over the brim and sloshed on the table. Frances was scowling at me.

"So sorry," she said to Aretha, without removing her hurt, gray eyes from mine. "What'll it be?"

Aretha asked for a Linzer tart, and I said that just the coffee was fine. Since I had been driving taxi I stopped in there from time to time because they had a pour-your-own coffee urn right at the cash register and only charged cab drivers a quarter—another thing you could have for a quarter in San Francisco. Frances was the waitress on the midnight shift, a sweet girl with a sadly pockmarked face and a drinking problem. We had a little routine going which involved my telling her that I had inherited vast wealth and was driving a taxi to express my solidarity with the working classes.

A moment later Frances returned, offhanding a cheese

Danish in front of Aretha as she passed by toward a table of Japanese businessmen who were sitting near the window and making loud but unintelligible remarks about the streetwalkers on parade outside the plate glass.

"Delightful girl," Aretha said.

"Aw, she's okay. Daughter of the Burroughs fortune, Wellesley summa cum laude, doing a doctoral dissertation on the warm-beverage preferences of people awake after midnight. There are a lot of very subtle correlations that would probably go right by you."

"They already have. Well, Henry. It's true after all? You *are* a cabbie. I mean I heard it but I thought no, no way. And then I thought, oh, it would be just like him. Just like you. But then I thought, well, it's an experience. Scraps of dialogue, slices of life. That kind of thing you're so good at. A taxicab. Oh, I could just see it, y'know, on a book jacket. 'Ben Henry drives a cab in Frisco.' Well, fill me in, Henry, what's it *really* like?"

"It's a living, Reeth, that's about all. I thought, before, you know, that I knew pretty much what there was to know about the city, but I found out that all I knew about, really, were the people who make the news and report it: reporters, politicians, cops, criminals. Now I know a lot more about the people who just read the news, or don't care about any of it at all. I don't know, it can be pretty grim and then something will happen. Like the other night I picked up a real old lady who gets drunk every night, *every* night, and drove her home. She said her husband was dead twenty years. I had to carry her to her door. It had been a long time since she bathed. I unlocked the door for her and put her on the couch in the living room. There must have been fifty cats in this sad little bungalow way down near the county line, a neighborhood I never even knew was there—have you ever been on Persia Avenue, or Moscow, Brazil, Peru, London, there's a whole neighborhood full of them, Italy—anyway, she roused herself long enough to pay me. You know what she said? She said, 'If I was thirty years younger I'd ask you in.' "

"What did you say?"

"Oh, I don't know, something like, 'I'm sorry I missed my chance.' You know what a cab driver would ask if I told him the same story? He'd say, 'Yeah? What did she tip?' "

"Isn't it dangerous? Aren't you scared?"

"Well, you hope you can trust your own judgment. As long as you're not stupid it's probably not a whole lot more dangerous than taking a walk at night."

"You must eavesdrop?"

"Actually I heard one about your boss." Aretha Palladine was the society editor of *The Courier* and one of the town's great gossips.

"A really bad one?" There was something saucy about her that I found likable. "You all know how I positively hate to hear about my boss's unwashed long johns." Her eyebrows had been plucked and then penciled, her eyelashes curled and darkened, and her eyeliner was black above and a shade of purple-blue below. She batted her long eyelids twice, slowly.

I laughed appreciatively. She smiled coyly, then giggled. "It's nice to see you, Henry," she said.

"It's nice to see you, too, Reeth. How's it goin'?"

"Now don't go changing the subject on me, Henry, I'm not one of those floozies you can set to panting with your excessive boyish charm and gritty urban cynicism and make 'em forget themselves. I want to hear the nasties about Thiesmann. You really ought to have your hair cut, you know? Don't you ever brush it?"

"This is just the way it is. It doesn't stay in place, doesn't matter if I comb it or not. I do, by the way. Listen, it was too bad about Shugart, wasn't it?"

"Oh Christ. Poor fucking Harry."

"I knew you were friends, I'm sorry. But, listen, Reeth, I'm going to tell you something that's got to be just between us." With Harry Shugart gone the best way to start a rumor going in San Francisco was to tell Aretha Palladine. She spent eight hours a day on the phone chatting up everybody who counted, and eight hours a night mingling. "I hear that Thiesmann may be under suspicion in the Shugart killing, for murdering Harry."

"What kind of bullshit is that? You can't be serious. You heard this in the taxicab?"

I wanted her to believe it might really be true. "It was an investigator in the D.A.'s office trying to impress a date. I asked some questions down at the Hall and it sounds like maybe there's something to it."

"Oh, that's funny, isn't it? I mean, that's hilarious. I mean what does the headline say if they bust the publisher of *The Courier* for murdering the columnist for *The Bulletin*?"

"How about: Arrest in Slaying Case Termed Unfounded? Mazer'll run it below the fold."

"Yeah, that's good. And *The Bulletin* says, eight columns, page one, Slayer of Bulletin's Shugart Arrested. Publisher of Morning Paper Free on Bail."

"How's your Danish?"

"Dry, day old. Definitely not a Linzer tart. But *why* would Thiesmann kill Harry Shugart?"

"What about young Ricky?"

"He's just a flit, what's he got to do with it? Oh, I see what you mean. Well, I don't know, that's a story that's been around for ages. Why should Thiesmann *père* do something about it now?"

"Maybe Ricky got knocked up."

"Hey, wait a minute, Henry. Did you get me here to confirm this for you? You cad." She was enjoying herself, which was no surprise. Gossip was stock-in-trade not just for her but for all newspaper people, and now that I thought of it, that was what had made Shugart so good: with considerable wit he reduced the form to its essence. "You're using *me* as your second source. Who are you writing for? Oh, you're a real bastard, you know that, Henry?" She batted her eyelids again. "I mean, what could I think when a guy invites me out for stale Danish and watery coffee at one in the morning? I could hardly not be expected to entertain certain thoughts . . ."

"But seriously."

"Seriously? True, it's been around for ages that little Ricky and Harry were maybe a thing, but y'all know, with Harry in the closet—I mean, *you* know, the fag baiting in the column and everything—I mean, who knows? Not this girl, uh-uh." She sipped her coffee and snapped open her evening bag to take out one of those mentholated you've-come-a-long-way-baby smokes, waiting for me to light it. Aretha had a tiny valentine-shaped mouth, brightly painted. When her cigarette was lit she exhaled and said, "It's plausible, isn't it?"

Within twenty-four hours all the people in San Francisco who thought of themselves as being the ones who counted would have heard that the cops suspected Thiesmann of killing Shugart because of the liaison between the columnist and the publisher's hairdresser son. Maybe even Thiesmann himself would have heard. Stir things up a little. Then again, would anybody care? San Francisco was a puzzlingly indifferent town. It had all the cosmopolitan trappings and a cheering section that had been led by Harry Shugart, but when you got right down to it, it was a small town. Heart and soul it was more like Cincinnati than it could ever admit to itself, a vain little popinjay of a town that called itself everybody's favorite. If it hadn't been so prettily located nobody would come to visit it. I think the Chamber of Commerce seriously believed the hills and the bay and the sparkling climate were the results of God's gratitude for sensible investment policies and a favorable business climate.

Our cups were empty and Frances was nowhere to be seen, so I walked over and refilled them myself. "Aretha," I said, when I got back to our table, "do you know some jerk named Jerry Cole?"

"The pilot. Upward Bound. Send a Poor Boy to Opening Night at the Opera. More or less linked with Harry's daughter. Just lately there's been talk of an impending nuptial. A deserving match, if you ask me. Let's see, he operates a charter service somewhere on the Peninsula. Half Moon Bay, Redwood City, I'm not certain where. I've flown with him, I was with Harry actually, on our way to a tennis weekend at John Gardiner's place. Airborne ferryman for some of the best people. My impression? That he aspires to be the next Bernie Shaw.''

"The playwright?''

"No, silly, the husband—the bodyguard who married Patricia Hearst. That gives Cole a motive, too, *naturellement*. Of course Harry isn't—wasn't—worth anything like Hearst.''

"It does, doesn't it? What was Harry's attitude toward Jerry Cole?''

"He didn't like him. Cole acted as if they were already related, and you could see Harry was cool on it. Frosty. It was kind of strained. But, listen, Henry, I'm not interested in Jerry Cole, I'm interested in you. Why were you sacked?''

"You'd have to ask that arrogant Brahmin who inherited a newspaper from his daddy.''

"Forget the class struggle, Henry. What happened?''

"I don't really know. I gave Mazer a memo about the investigation I was doing, cops and drug dealers and some other stuff like that—it was the best work I ever did for them—and the next thing I know Mazer is telling me Thiesmann's fired me. He had Mazer tell me I was careless, reckless. A disgrace to the profession.'' It was not easy to get the words out.

"Why does it bother you so much? Was it true?''

"That's a hell of a thing to say. Goddamn it, Reeth, don't get psychological on me, okay?''

"It's your life, Henry, but if you ask me you should be asking yourself why you're so goddamn angry that you're ready to slug *me*!''

"It's not you I want to slug.'' A sudden wave of dizziness wrapped itself around my forehead but passed. "Isn't it obvious why I'm angry? I mean I was fired. You know what the worst part was? He wouldn't talk to me himself, he had Mazer do his dirty work for him.''

"He's not your father, he's your publisher.''

"Someday I'm going to rub his face in it.''

"You big sap, don't you get the message? If you insist

on being a germ you'll be quarantined before you cause an epidemic. You barged around *The Courier* as if *you* owned the place, and you *were* careless sometimes, weren't you? It's not your ball, Henry, and you can't play in the game unless you play by the rules. At least most of the time. You offended Thiesmann because you weren't smart enough to pretend to respect him. And you scare him, too. You see?''

"You really think he was right to fire me?"

"Poor baby," Aretha said. She stroked my cheek.

"Everything okay here?" Frances had appeared out of nowhere.

Aretha smiled knowingly and reached into her evening bag for her compact. She examined herself in the mirror, applying a little powder to her upturned button nose and primping her dark bangs.

"Hey, we're fine, Frances. Thanks."

"I'll bet." She turned on her heel.

"What *is* that girl's claim on you, Henry?"

"None at all. I mean, I have coffee in here sometimes, we kid around."

"Are you going to Harry's funeral?"

I shook my head. "I hardly knew the man."

"I loved him. Seriously, Henry, don't say anything smartass, but he was a bastard. Sentimental like the truly cold-hearted usually are. He would wear spiked golf shoes to walk over the back of anybody he didn't fear himself, and prostrate himself in front of anybody with enough money or power or style to impress him suitably. He was one of those men, y'know, who got tears in his eyes when he talked about his daughter but never had time to take her to the circus when she was little? But I loved him because he knew who he was and what he wanted and he thrived on his success. He was the best, wasn't he, Henry? The very best at what we do." I could see the dampness behind her eyes. Then she brightened, but her eyes were still damp. "Nobody but nobody in this town dared not to have him on their A-list, and nobody let him pick up a check. You see, Henry, he was deep down cheap and he was more than a success, he was a triumph.''

There was a longish silence between us during which I wondered if a truly cheap guy would be buying a quarter of a pound of cocaine, and if he would, why? That is, if Yollo had been telling me the truth, which was another question. Or even if Shugart were so tightfisted his daughter might be in want of an independent income.

Finally Aretha left a ten-dollar bill on the Formica table next to her nibbled-at Danish, and when I objected she said, ''Expense account. On Thiesmann.'' Frances came over with the check; it couldn't have been more than three bucks, and Aretha waved a hand, dismissing the check and the change.

''You've got the most wonderful tarts in here, dear.'' Aretha was out the door before Frances or I had time to react.

''Why do you have to bring other women in here?'' Frances hissed.

''It was work,'' I said. ''Damn it, Frances, you and I hardly know each other.''

''Hah!'' she said and walked away, leaving me standing there with two different women heading in two different directions, both out-of-sorts with me. How had I managed that?

I caught up with Aretha where she was waiting on the sidewalk, looking like a chicken in the fox coop among the bag ladies and hookers and cowboys from another planet who were on this part of Geary Street at this tired time of the morning. A taxi driver cruising by slowed down and looked inquiringly at us. Aretha never noticed, but I waved him off.

''God, Aretha, that wasn't necessary.''

''So little is, baby, and the little bit that is is just exactly what you refuse to understand.'' She put a small hand up to my cheek and kissed me lightly on the lips. ''I'm not mad at you, Henry, don't mope.''

''You'll remember not to repeat what I told you about Thiesmann, right?''

"Strictly *entre nous*."

I offered her a lift but she had her car stashed across the street with the doorman of the Clift Hotel, so I walked her that far before we parted ways. A few minutes later I parked in my usual spot in Adler Alley and went upstairs and called the service.

"Oh, hello, Ben," Peter answered. "You have some messages here."

"Hi, Peter. How's your night going?"

"It is not a bad night, Ben. Monday is never a bad night because the tapes are new at Dial-A-Story and Dial-A-Rumor."

"Is that how you pass the wee hours, Peter, making phone calls to tapes?"

"There are so many free places to call, Ben. This is what is so wonderful about America." Peter was Belgian, in the country illegally on a long-expired tourist visa. "I had the nicest talk tonight, Ben, with the people at the suicide hotline. They are so supportive, Ben. They are the most together people there."

"Don't need 'em yet, Peter."

"Oh, good, that's good. I had a good talk with your wife, too, Ben. She is really so worried about her bills; you should send her the money you owe. It's so awful to be worried like that."

"Good Christ, Peter. Did anybody call besides Lottie? And she's my former wife."

"Yes, Ben. Let's see. One from a Miss Judy Shugart. She says she would like to meet with you, you have the number. Oh, yes, here's another one, do you have a pencil, Ben? This next one is extremely weird. This chap, he made me write it down exactly as he says it. Are you ready? Here goes. 'Not Buddy. Laughing Sal's place.' That's *es ay el*, Ben, Sal's place. 'Delivery hour. Tuesday.' Do you understand that, Ben? Because I do not."

"Not all of it. Laughing Sal's place? Oh, yeah, okay, Peter, I get it." Laughing Sal had been a mechanical fat lady with a haunting cackle at Playland-at-the-Beach before the amusement park had been torn down to make way for a hole in the ground. "That all the messages?"

"Yes, Ben. I do not know what this Laughing Sal is referring to, but you should be careful. That man who calls himself Not Buddy, Ben, I get negative vibes from him."

8

What sort of man is it who harnesses the frenetic energy of renewed purpose to a Hoover upright? I jammed the vacuum as far under my overstuffed chair as it would go. I had already put fresh sheets on the bed, washed the dishes, wiped the counter, swept, dusted, and thrown out the trash, including the evening paper where I had read that Inspector F. D. R. Pressix was closing in on the suspected killers of Harry Shugart. In other words, nothing to report. Only Shugart himself could have made it readable: "Around the Hall of Justice they're whispering about the gilded cages the cops are rattling. One offended newspaper executive pelted the Gendarme with United Fruit Company stock certificates." Earlier in the day I had given Vince a whack at my shaggy head, brought my laundry round to the Chinese lady, and finally mailed Lottie her check, resisting the impulse to post it without a stamp the way she and I had mailed our telephone and utility bills back when we were hellbent on bankrupting the capitalist system in fifteen-cent increments. And now I was Hoovering, Hoovering frantically against the impossible chance that my mother would pop in, God rest her spic 'n span soul.

The question persisted: what kind of man? Since I lived alone I had become compulsively tidy. It was a quick and painless way to achieve visible results. Bim bam, thank you Ben. The clean and tidy surroundings reflected well on me and diverted attention, especially my own, away from a life that was otherwise cluttered with nothing. Soon maybe I would have something better than a good Hoovering to look forward to. It was damn near a joy to have a head full of questions about something other than myself, and in a few hours I would be meeting Yollo and getting some answers. That was number one, the work I was doing, whatever it was. I flicked off the Hoover, wrapped the cord around it, and put it away in the kitchen broom closet. Number two involved the small sheet of notepad paper beside the telephone.

She answered the first ring.

"Who is it?" Cross.

"Hello, Ben Henry."

"What do you want?"

This was not the reception I had been trying not to imagine all day long. "I'm returning your call. You left a message."

"Well, forget it, will you."

"Gladly."

We both hung up. I stood there a minute looking over my clean and tidy apartment. Then I slammed my fist against the wall hard enough to buckle the plaster.

At Tosca's I downed two quick vodkas before I switched to beer, smoking and brooding. I arranged the crumbs of a *cialda*, an Italian sweet biscuit, into a neat pile on the bar top and then blew them to kingdom come with a flick of my finger. A line from an old song kept running through my head: Luck, be a lady tonight. Not good. Joseph poured the last of my Beck's into my glass and asked me if I wanted another.

"Speaking of luck," I said when he brought the fresh bottle, "have you ever noticed that there's no number thirteen in San Francisco? They call Thirteenth Avenue Funston and Thirteenth Street Duboce."

"Like on elevators," Joseph said.

"Yeah. Funston was the general in charge of executing looters after the earthquake. I can understand how they were feeling pretty superstitious right then. But when you come right down to it, what's the point? You can call it any damn thing you want but it's still the thirteenth.''

He considered that for a moment, picking up an already clean glass and wiping it thoughtfully. "I see what you mean," he finally said. "God's nobody's fool.''

"That's what makes him different from you and me."

A little while later I was driving toward Ocean Beach, with the excitement tap-dancing on my nerves, and the liquor turning cartwheels through my mind. This was not the best condition in which to be meeting a hunted man in possession of $90,000 worth of cocaine who was possibly implicated in a murder. And a poor place as well. The nearer I got to the ocean the thicker the fog became, the more steeply the pine and cypress trees in the darkened park bent to the wind. An involuntary chill ran down my spine, so I rolled up the car window, turned on the heater, and set the windshield wipers to clearing the obscuring mist. The wipers slapped into action while my tires sucked at the damp road.

When you reach the last rise in the road at Point Lobos Boulevard the miles of Ocean Beach spread out below you all the way to the horizon, but in the dark I couldn't see any further than where the beams from my headlights stopped penetrating the fog. I heard the pounding of the surf and the cries of the sea lions on the offshore rocks as I drove past the baroque Cliff House down the steep incline toward the sea. I wasn't sanguine about mucking around among desperate people like Yollo and whoever was after him when I was so ignorant of the facts. Sensing a presence I looked in my rearview mirror, but no headlights showed behind me. Jumpy nerves.

I rolled to a cautious stop in front of what had once been Playland-at-the-Beach, the domain of Laughing Sal. The huckster who had bought the amusement park had ripped it down and left this gash of sandswept earth and rubble as his legacy, a debris-strewn urban grave, under which was buried the laughter of children. He had planned to build something there, condos most likely, but his financing collapsed. They said he was a man with no navel. What he had done, the man with no navel, was wicked, but it wasn't surprising that it had been allowed in San Francisco, which was a town that turned its back on little kids, the worst city in the country for raising a family.

The motorcycle made a barely audible whine at first, a sound that grew louder and louder as the machine approached from the south. I had kept my amber parking lights on, and now I lit a Danneman and waited. The motorcycle went right by without slowing so I thought it wasn't Yollo after all, but then a few hundred feet along he evidently made a U-turn, because he emerged again from the fog to my north and pulled up beside me. He got off his bike without removing his helmet and walked over, his arms hanging and his palms up. In his bulky down vest and thick gloves he looked like a stuffed teddy bear from Mars. He flipped his visor.

"Top of the evening," he said, as sardonic as usual.

"I've just been sitting here ruing Playland. Have you ever heard about the Ferris brothers?"

"Should I be acquainted with them?"

"Well, they're amusing, that's all. One of them invented the wheel, the Ferris wheel. His brother popped the first popcorn, he was summoned to do a command performance by Queen Victoria."

Without responding he looked over his shoulder and then into the fogbound darkness beyond my car. Nothing stirred along the flat stretch of beach front except for the waves beyond the sea wall, which whooshed and slammed against the beach. Now and then a gull cried. "What have you found out?"

"The police want you for questioning. They seem to regard you as a suspect."

"You're quite certain?"

I nodded.

"Already," he said. "Well, the other side doesn't hold trials."

"You are much sought after."

He looked over his shoulder again. "You took care not to be followed, Benjamin?"

"Yeah, I was careful. You didn't kill Shugart, did you?"

He seemed startled that I had asked. "No. Do you believe me?"

"Mostly," I told him truthfully. "Have you considered turning yourself in and letting them question you? Hell, there's nothing they can charge you with."

"No. I'm safer where I am than I would be among that pack of common criminals in the jail."

"Well, you've got a point, but if you change your mind I'd be willing to be your go-between."

"What other pearls have you scooped up?"

"Enough so that I doubt Harry Shugart was the buyer of the coke."

"Does it really matter, dear boy?"

"If you want any more help from me it does."

"I never exactly said it was Shugart. I was most precise."

"Fine," I said and turned on my motor.

"Don't act so rashly, Benjamin. What's the matter?"

"Cut out the guessing games, Yollo. You're in trouble, and I get the feeling that if I keep poking around I'm going to be in trouble too. Level with me. Did you see Thiesmann there that night?"

We both turned toward the sound of a car approaching. After a moment its headlights stabbed the fog from the north, the direction from which I had come. It came toward us slowly, the driver apparently inching his way through the dense, wet night.

"I may have," Yollo said, keeping a wary eye on the approaching headlights. "Somebody in a midnight blue Jaguar XJ6 was pulling away just as I first arrived, but I didn't stop to get a look. It was not to my advantage to be seen myself. I took evasive action and returned rather cautiously."

I was about to ask Yollo again about whether Shugart was his buyer when there was a brilliant flash of fire from the window of the car I had ceased to watch. Yollo seemed to rise up on his tiptoes and then he fell, sinking below my open window. He let out a horrible sound, a shriek that drowned in his throat.

"Buddy!" I screamed. Buddy, not Yollo. Buddy, I'm sorry, man.

The other car was already streaking south, enveloped by the fog. What make or model had it been? Long, dark, late model, that was all I had seen. I shoved against my door but Yollo's weight slumped against it was too great to dislodge. It took a tremendous effort to push open the door, and as I did he rolled away from the car onto the asphalt. I could see he was dead. What had been a man a few breaths ago was now a lump of flesh on the wet ground.

My heart wanted to flee my rib cage as I bent over him, zipped open his vest, and felt for a heartbeat. There was none. He had breasts like a woman. I leaned into my car to turn on the headlights, took hold of Yollo under his armpits, and dragged him into the glare of the lights, keeping a lookout for the assassin's car in case it returned. I wrenched off Yollo's helmet. Blood was staining the front of his shirt; there seemed to be a wound in his throat. I wasn't about to wipe the thick, warm blood to get a closer look. I had never seen anybody killed before and what I could not get over was how fast a man died, a blink that became an eternity. I wanted to get out of there.

I left his body where it lay and started back toward North Beach, pounding the dashboard and shouting curses. From time to time I looked to see if I was being followed, but now I knew I probably wouldn't know it if I were. The killer had come from the north, the same direction from which I had arrived. My carelessness had cost Yollo his life.

Careless! Damn it, the satchel. I hadn't looked for it and I didn't know if Yollo had it with him when he was murdered. *Why* hadn't I looked? Was I really as careless as Thiesmann had said? I considered going back. But why bother? It certainly was more dangerous than it was valuable. No way, $90,000 worth of cocaine was not enough to send me back out there to Yollo Current's corpse. Damn it! I banged the dashboard again and turned around.

Yollo and his bike were exactly where I had left them, and nobody else seemed to be about. I got out of my car and approached the bike cautiously. The carrier rack was empty, but the straps were undone. Unless Yollo had driven to the beach with the buckles banging, somebody had already been there and removed the satchel.

When I got back to my place—the care I had taken to tidy it now a double mockery—I called police operations. Without saying who I was I told them where they would find Yollo Current—I had to spell his name twice—and that Inspector Pressix in Homicide would want to know.

A few minutes later the phone rang abruptly, making me jump. It was past two in the morning, and I wasn't expecting any callers.

"Hello," she said. "This is Judy. I didn't wake you, did I?"

All I said was "No."

"You're right to be mad at me. I couldn't talk before, I was having an awful fight with Jerry when you called and he was right there."

"I see." I eyed the dent in the plaster, felt the corresponding ache in my ego.

"C'mon, give me a chance to make it up to you. I want to buy you a drink. I know what you must be thinking, but I'm just a dumb girl. Really, don't be angry with me. I need your help, there are things I'm finding out that scare me."

I felt nothing, absolutely nothing. "You know Tosca's?" I asked her. "Meet me there tomorrow night at eleven."

"Tosca's, okay."

I hung up and then put my jacket back on and slowly followed my feet downstairs and out to the car again. I needed to talk to somebody, and when it was this bad there was only Buddy.

9

It had surprised me when I learned that Buddy had prepared a will and stunned me to hear that he had left his house to me. The house wasn't much to look at, a wood frame cottage near the end of a short unpaved road at the eastern base of Potrero Hill abutting the Southern Pacific tracks with only one other house nearby, the Hell's Angels clubhouse. After the Gold Rush the area had been settled mostly by Russian immigrants, and much of the land had once been pasture. Now it was rundown enough to warrant its name, Dogpatch. I hadn't the heart to sell Buddy's house, or to rent it out. Living in it was unthinkable.

I don't think Buddy had made out a will because he was a careful man, although he was; nor because he cared one way or another what happened to his worldly goods after he was gone. No, I believe Buddy had prepared a will as a way of looking straight into the eyes of his sense of doom. Over the years Buddy had lost faith in everything, everything, that is, except the value of relieving other people's pain. He had begun, increasingly, to dress in black, and he had grown a beard that covered his cheekbones and obscured his face except for his eyes, which had lost their sense of amusement and finally lost even their sympathy until they were usually indwelling, looking in toward a wasteland beyond my powers of comprehension. He had once been robust, given to frenzies of loud joy, tromping through the mountains under the weight of a fifty-pound pack singing Wagner, but in the last year of his life he had become gaunt and lifeless. He imagined offenses where none existed, trusted nobody, and finally reached an exquisite state of paranoid suspicion. In the months before he died he had become as alone as a man can make himself. All that kept him going, it seemed, was his practice at the clinic where he tended the pains and sorrows of the people who lived in the housing projects that clung to the slopes of the hill west of the railroad tracks. They were nasty projects where a man was white before he was a man, and I never took calls up there in the taxi. Buddy ministered to those people heart and soul, in sickness and often in death. After he was murdered Lottie wrote a poem about him, a line of which I would never forget: "Maybe his daily trysts with death wounded him in the end."

It had been a fine summer day, warm and clear, when an old Russian who also lived like a hermit had come into the clinic complaining of severe chest pains. Buddy put aside what he was doing and saw him immediately. When they were alone Boris Mayevsky pulled out a gun and shot Buddy twice in the head at close range. I hope he died immediately, before he had time to reflect on the siren song he had sung to lure death into his examining room. Mayevsky turned the gun against himself so there would never be a satisfactory explanation for why he had murdered Buddy, but searching medical records at the clinic the police found an old file on Mayevsky's sister, who had been under Buddy's care when she was dying of cancer. Buddy had visited her regularly in the home she shared with her brother, and one entry seemed to be the only penlight into the darkness. "Trouble with M. today. He seemed to think I'm responsible for Shirley willing her money to charity. What to do?" Of course there wouldn't even have been that meager clue if Buddy hadn't been the kind of doctor to concern himself with the emotional state of his patient's family. I could never shake the conviction that the mad old man was mated to Buddy in some dark ritual of the psyche.

I unlocked the door and saw immediately that some-body had been there, had been living there. In the light cast through a thin curtain by a street lamp I could see dishes and utensils on the table where a meal had been eaten, and when I stepped forward my foot struck a soft bundle on the floor. I groped for the light switch, my body poised and my mind tense, searching for movement in the dark corners of the room. I found the switch, flooding the room with light. At my feet was a duffel bag with clothes spilling out of it. Strewn across the floor were the news-papers from the last week, opened to the stories about Harry Shugart's death. On the table beside the dishes were a scale and a mirror. Yollo. This was where Yollo had been hiding out.

I walked over and tinkled a couple of keys on the piano. I kept going into the bedroom and sat down in Buddy's swivel chair at his desk and turned on the desk lamp. Clipped to the shade was a message he had found inside a Chinese fortune cookie: "There's many a good man to be found beneath a shabby hat." The corny sentiment had once been so much like him. I rolled the chair over to the bed and picked up his basketball in both my hands and tossed it thoughtfully over my lap. Buddy was a bruising player with a surprisingly soft touch on his fallaway jump shot, and we had been an even match.

"Battles," I said out loud. "We fought battles, baby, and I never could have stayed with you if you didn't give it away when you were going to go right by sticking your tongue out of the right side of your mouth. I never told you that, did I, amigo? You tipped your hand, Buddy, you gave it away. Gave it away every time."

I wiped my eyes and blew my nose. The basketball slid to the floor and rolled up against a bookcase.

"I really fucked up, Buddy. That's nothing new, huh? I'm sorry about what happened to Yollo. It was my fault, and I'm sorry as hell."

If Buddy had been alive, the Buddy who still had faith, I know what he would have done and said. He would have grasped my wrist and looked right into my eyes, absorbed my pain because his eyes had once been sponges for other people's hurt. *No, it wasn't, Sleuth. He wouldn't have been out there if he wasn't dealing. The dangers were what he chose, not you.*

"Still, I was careless, drunk—well, not sober, anyway—and feeling bad for myself because a beautiful woman who made something move in me that hadn't moved in a long, long time gave me the cold shoulder. I'm lonely, I'm confused. I feel like I ruin what I touch."

You know what makes a champion, Benny?

"A champion? Yeah, he's better at what he does than everybody else."

No. No. He lasts one second longer. Tenacity. You put glass in his socks and he survives. He marches, stomp, stomp, stomp. He goes on.

"I got the feeling there near the end, Buddy, that you weren't a champion." That would have made him laugh. "But you had wisdom all the same."

Wisdom? That wasn't wisdom, Benny. That was living long enough to make every mistake known to man.

"You know what I'm thinking, Buddy? I'm thinking it's high time I made something of myself."

You're something already, Sleuth. You made it this far, didn't you?

"Yeah, but look what they're doing to me. Everything good gets wrecked. Lottie. My job. Even Yollo when I'm the only one he can come to."

Nobody did any of those things to you, Benny. You did 'em to yourself, every one of 'em. You're doing it to yourself and you don't even know what it is you're doing.

First one motorcycle, then two, three, four roared menacingly outside the Hell's Angels house, shaking me free of my reverie, or whatever it was. They took off, and I was once again sitting in an empty house that had been inhabited at one time and another by two men who had been murdered. I turned off the lamp and went back through the house toward the door, stopping only to rummage through Yollo's duffel bag. I found a small address book, which I dropped into my pocket, and his flute, which I brought over and laid on Buddy's piano.

I had the door open when I remembered what Buddy always said to me after I had brought him my troubles.

Don't let the bastards grind you down, Sleuth.

10

The fog was still in when I pulled into the parking lot at the Hall of Justice. F.D.R. Pressix was at his desk, pecking out a report on his typewriter. I lit a cigarette and waited, admiring the drape of his suit and the way his amber silk pocket handkerchief matched his tie. Finally he sighed and swiveled in his chair to face me. Nothing in his face moved. Controlled cynicism had formed his face into a huge, intimidating shield, a shield to warn onlookers that behind this large body backed up by a gun and a badge was an anger you provoked at your own great peril.

"What kind of gun was it that did the job on Yollo?"

"Waiting for ballistics," he said. "Look like somethin' small caliber. Thirty-two. What the hell you doin' comin' round to sass me, Sonny?"

"Whoever did him followed me out there. I had a feeling I was being followed but I didn't see anybody. I called it in, told them to let you know."

"Material witness," he said. "Why'd you depart from the scene?" He leaned back in his chair. I thought surely the wood would crack under his weight.

"I'm here now."

"Aidin' and abettin' a fugitive, too. Shovelin' your usual pile ear high. What brung you to meetin' the deceased way out there so late at night?"

"He wanted to talk. He had heard you wanted to question him about Shugart and he was scared and he wanted to know what was going on."

"Nice sort of fella, drug dealer."

"Yeah," I said acidly, "corrupting the morals of reporters and lawyers and advertising guys and sheriff's deputies. So what?"

"He youh dealer?"

"No, sir, Inspector. C'mon, man, what difference does that make now?"

Pressix grunted. Those great big mocha hands of his rested on his vested belly just above the silver badge he wore on his belt. I had the feeling I couldn't tell him anything he didn't really already know.

"See the perpetrators?" he asked me.

I shook my head. "It happened too fast. They were in a dark late-model sedan and they took off to the south along the Great Highway."

"They shoot at you?"

"No, one shot."

"Got any idea who it was?"

"Well, he told me he was in hiding because a deal had gone bad and there were some people he owed a lot of money to. Your narcotics people might know more about that, I imagine the word's around. In fact, if you get me some names I might be able to help you locate them." Yollo's address book was still in my pocket. I resisted the desire to touch it. As soon as I got around cops I felt like I had something to hide.

"What kind of deal would that be, cocaine?"

"You know what I'm wondering? I'm wondering how come you knew to be looking for him. About Shugart, I mean."

"Got a tip."

"Who from?"

"Confidential source."

"Listen, Franklin, I don't think Yollo killed Shugart. He was up there, but so were other people. It was goddamn rush hour. Judy Shugart was there and so was her boyfriend, Cole. And Thiesmann, you knew that, didn't you? Have you questioned him yet?''

For the first time his big face showed some feeling. It was an expression akin to the way a man looks when he gets a splinter under his skin, slightly pained and mightily annoyed.

"You sure you know what youh saying?" Pressix asked.

"Why don't you bring him down and ask him?''

"Don't really have no way of knowing he was there, do I? Don't want to disturb the man for nothin'.''

"You didn't have any way of knowing Yollo was there either except for a tip. Don't I count as a confidential source?''

Our eyes held. Finally he sighed and ran a huge hand over his head. There was a fringe of gray kinky hair around his ears and neck, but it was his bald pate that he stroked.

"Be around,'' he said. "I could be wantin' to talk to you some moah about this.'' He swiveled in his chair and went back to pecking out his report.

In the corridor outside Homicide I ran into Nellie Flynn, the regular police reporter for *The Courier*. Most reporters are shy egotists—the few who aren't shy become stars like Sam Donaldson or Shugart—and Nellie was no exception. Nellie and I were not friends, but he had helped me as much as he could with my investigations while still maintaining his good relations with the cops. We made the allowances we had to make for each other.

"Hey,'' he said. "Whatcha doing in white man's country, Tonto?'' Nellie's long thin nose was crisscrossed by red capillaries and his eyes when wide open barely admitted the light of day.

"Social call. How's it goin', Nellie?''

"Gingersnap. Circulation's up ten thousand since Shugart bought his one-way ticket.''

"What's new down at the funny paper?''

"You hear about Hubbel?''

"You mean the society decorator? The one in Shugart's crowd?''

Nellie nodded. "He fried a girl. Wrapped his car around

a tree doing 120 with a blood alcohol level off the charts.
Priors, too.''

"I didn't see it in the paper."

"And upset his mother's servants?" Nellie said. "Thiesmann knows how hard it is to find good help these days.''
He saluted and ambled off toward the Chief's office. It
must have been ten o'clock, time for the daily briefing, a
routine I had once followed as well. I didn't wait for the
elevator but took the stairs down to the lobby.

The San Francisco Gun Exchange is situated at the bor-
der of the city's financial district, as if guarding the back
door to where the money is kept. The walls of the Exchange bristled with rifles and shotguns in upright racks,
and the middle aisle was chockablock with ammo, hol-
sters, handbooks, and other shooters' doodads, but I went
directly to the long glass case where the handguns were
displayed. I walked slowly along the length of the case
looking at one gun after another without knowing any more
about each one than which end you held and which you
pointed.

There were a lot of men about my age—too young for
Korea and a whisker too old or too reluctant for Vietnam—
who had the happy misfortune never to have been in com-
bat. I say *happy* because any man who wants to shoot at
other people will sooner or later be shot at himself, and I
was not among them. I was no warrior, and my patriotism
wasn't of the combative variety. And yet it was also a
misfortune never to have been under fire, because a man
who doesn't know how he would react in a battle will
always harbor a secret doubt about his courage. I wasn't
there to prove to myself that I was brave. I had come to
the Exchange before in the grip of just such a silly conun-
drum and always walked out empty-handed and abashed.
But today I was here with a purpose. Whoever had murdered Yollo would have reason to shoot me too before I
was through, and I intended to fight back if it came to
that.

A mousy clerk with rounded shoulders, thin, sandy hair,

and frameless eyeglasses followed me for a few feet along the counter before he spoke. "Help ya?"

When I looked directly at him I saw from the tightness at the corners of his censorious mouth that he wasn't meek as he had first appeared.

"I'm looking for a gun."

"A house gun or a friend?"

"A what?"

He patted his narrow butt. "Somebody to keep you company, a friend."

"I have no experience with guns, but I want to be able to protect myself."

"I understand. I'd say a four-inch barrel on a thirty-eight revolver, no-frills type. Step down here." He led me back along the counter and stooped to unlock the case. On the glass counter between us he placed a chunky, oiled weapon.

"Now I recommend the thirty-eight because that's the most caliber a person who isn't a shooter by vocation or profession can generally handle well. But you're a big fella, I don't know. I recommend a no-frills type like this one because sights that're useful to a target shooter are no use whatever at fifteen feet or whatever the longest room in your house is."

I hefted the gun. It felt alien in my hand and heavier than I had expected. "This would do what to somebody if I shot them?"

"Kill 'em dead. Anytime you launch a projectile at someone you have to be prepared for taking his life. Y'see, I could acquaint you with a thirty-two, but a thirty-eight stops fights better. When you use a gun to protect yourself it's my opinion that you have to get this thing about not taking a life out of your head. My personal philosophy, see, is if I ever need a gun to defend myself I simply just don't care if my attacker survives or not."

"This thirty-eight is a heavy piece of machinery. It's unwieldy." I pointed at a smaller, flatter weapon under the glass, oiled to a lustrous blue-gray finish. "What about that one?"

"Now that takes a clip instead of cartridges," he said. "The Walther PPK-S, three-and-a-half inches." He handed it to me. It was lighter and more comfortable in my hand.

A Walther. Why did that ring a bell? "Isn't this . . ."

"Right, James Bond."

"Aha, right. And this has the same fight-stopping potential as the thirty-eight?"

"Well, it's not as powerful as the thirty-eight. But it'll kill 'em too."

What had always been a figure of speech to me, even when I had seen corpses on the coroner's slab or went over a murder scene with a cop, had in the course of less than a week become this substantial hunk of metal I was thoughtfully weighing against my palm. I had never particularly liked either Harry Shugart or Yollo Current, but their deaths had changed my life as suddenly and irrevocably as a draft notice.

"I'll take the Walther," I told him.

"A good choice," he said, and then busied himself with receipts and permit applications. When that was finished he helped me pick out a holster and taught me how to load and eject the seven-shell clip, how the safety worked, how to aim. As I was leaving he said, "Well, you achieved a friend. Congratulations."

11

I cruised Montgomery Street through the embankments of bleak fortresses, the banks, brokerage houses, law offices, insurance companies, the buyers and sellers of the future, looking for a fare and listening with half an ear to Doris as well as to the Giants on the radio. I wasn't nearly as intent as I had been only a week before on making every penny I could in the taxi because I was thinking about what to do next. I was thinking like a reporter and yet I wasn't at all. Doing an investigation as a reporter I had thought about getting the story. The tug was much the same: a harpoon had been set under my skin and I would follow wherever it pulled. When you were a reporter, though, you began with the question "What's the story?" and if you kept going, sooner or later you ended up with enough to write. The news story you wrote was as rigidly contained within a formula as a haiku. I felt like a microbiologist who one day throws away his microscope and enrolls in medical school, decides to study the whole organism instead of its cellular makeup. The question now was: what happened?

There was another difference, too. As a reporter I received a weekly paycheck, signed by Richard C. Thiessmann II. As whatever kind of sleuth I was now, my pay came to nil. I lowered the volume of the ball game and turned Doris up louder on the dispatch radio. Gotta make a buck. Though they put glass in my shoes, I will keep my foot to the pedal. The possibility of just walking away from the question of what was behind the deaths of Harry Shugart and Yollo Current certainly existed—with Yollo dead there was nothing to stop me—but I was going on because nobody else would, certainly not the newspapers and probably not Pressix. Somebody had to care enough to find out. Tug. I nominate me. Elected by acclaim since there are no other nominees. Thank you very much. I accept the obligation as being entirely mine. Obligation. I had walked away from my obligations before, and though it had taken years to decide it was what I must do, and though I didn't regret what I had done, I would never entirely get over having done it, nor would Lottie.

Before I knew it I was driving south on the Junipero Serra Freeway along a familiar route, remembering. I had arrived at the university a month before my eighteenth birthday and two months before John Kennedy was assassinated in Dallas. When I heard the news I took my basketball and went to a public schoolyard near the campus. I had been alone there except for a Negro boy. For a while we both shot and rebounded at opposite ends of a concrete court, but when his ball came off the rim at an angle that rocketed it over his head toward me, I retrieved it and asked him if he wanted a game. He nodded. I passed the ball to him. "Your outs," I said, and that was the last time we spoke. We played hard for a long time until we were both drenched with sweat—the Negro boy's head and face looked like he had been caught in a thunderstorm—even though the air was cold. It was the only basketball game I had ever played in where neither side showed any interest in keeping score. We played until dark and then I walked back to campus. I wanted to be around people but I didn't want to talk. When I went into the campus coffeehouse it was jammed with students and faculty, but strangely quiet. I kept my eyes down and looked for a place to sit where I wouldn't be forced to acknowledge anybody—it seemed that to have talked would have been to diminish the feeling—and I ended up beside a girl who was sitting alone, fighting back tears. She was wearing a black cashmere sweater over a round collar blouse. She had very large eyes and dark brows and a face that seemed exceptionally soft and gentle. She wore her hair long and straight. Without any hesitation I sat down and said to her, "I never felt so alone in my entire life." She looked at me full in the face and then her composure crumbled and she began to sob. I took her hand and we sat there quietly for a long, long time. Two weeks later we made love, the first time for both of us. Two months later we were married.

I pulled up in front of our house. Strike that. In front of Lottie's house. I kept the motor running and listened to the Giants go down without threatening in the sixth inning, trailing 4–2. I was certain they were going to lose. Being a Giants fan, it was hard not to feel that way. It was the second time I had been back to this modest bungalow we had bought because we both liked the fog, and once upon a time Pacifica had seemed like a good place to raise the kids we were planning to have; the first time I had come when Lottie was out and hauled away my stuff.

The lawn had gone to hell, left scorched and patchy by the drought and neglect. The sprinkler I had bought at Sears lay rusted on its side near where the nasturtium bed had been. I paused before I knocked. Through the door I heard a record playing, one of those indistinguishable woman folk singers, Holly Near maybe. To me Holly Near was pretty much a generic term.

Lottie kept the chain latched when she opened the door. "Jesus," she said through the crack. "What are you doing here?"

"I really don't know. I felt bad about being late with the payment and I just happened to be in the neighborhood so I thought I'd drop by and make sure you got it. It arrived okay?"

"This morning."

Somewhere behind her a man's voice asked, "Is everything all right? Who is it?"

"Oops," I said.

"Wait a minute." She left the door ajar and the chain

latched and went into the living room. I could hear voices, low voices, his quizzical, hers urgent and reassuring. When she returned she released the chain and I followed her inside.

"Ben Henry," she said. "Carl Ivens."

He was stocky and had a full beard that was shot through with gray. He looked very comfortable there on the old divan we had bought at a yard sale and reupholstered ourselves, working all one weekend to replace the springs. His shoes were off and his stockinged feet were resting on the leathertop coffee table. There were cigarette scars on the round leather surface and a vase of dried flowers. I could have told you how every one of the burns got there.

"I've heard a lot about you," he said, wanting to be friendly.

"Yeah." I couldn't think of what to say next. He seemed forthright and certainly less ill at ease then either Lottie or I were. They had been smoking a joint; I could smell its acrid sweetness. The folksinger was still singing. "I didn't mean to barge in on you like this."

"No problem," Carl said. "I was getting restless, a walk would do me good. You probably have some stuff to talk over, right?" He got up—his pot belly looked hard but it still surprised me, Lottie had always liked skinny guys—and slipped his feet into handmade sandals. Then he came over and offered his hand. He was shorter than me and balding. "Nice to meet you," he said, turning to Lottie as our hands parted.

I could tell he wanted to touch her but held himself back. "See you in a while. Have a good talk." He smiled to reassure her. She took his arm—that pleased him—and whispered something as she walked him to the door.

When he opened it I called out, "Carl!" Lottie spun toward me expecting the worst. Her look warned me: don't you dare, you bastard. But she didn't understand.

"Thanks," I said.

He waved a hand in my direction. His other hand was on the knob, the door wide open. "That your cab?" he asked.

I nodded.

"Well, it looks like a great night for a walk," he said and shut the door behind him.

I reached for a Danneman but stopped in midmotion, remembering how Lottie hated the smell of cigars. "He seems like a good guy," I said.

"I know that. What are you doing here?" I hadn't seen her in many months and I searched her for signs of change. She was dressed like a gypsy, a new style for her, in a colorful scarf and billowing accordion pants and a tentlike blouse the colors of parrots. There were small scars hidden in the pucker beneath her left eye and on her chin from gashes she had suffered in an auto accident not long before our marriage collapsed from exhaustion, vestiges of pain that I could never look at without feeling all the wounds we had inflicted on each other. I had left her in the end because it finally came to seem like the lesser cruelty. I could not bear hurting her but I did every day I stayed where I didn't want to be.

"I really don't know. I was thinking about obligations. Not about you and me at first, actually. Somebody I was trying to help was murdered. I felt responsible. Do you remember Yollo Current?"

"That fat little pig of a woman-hating grass dealer?"

"That's the one, Buddy's ward. He was murdered out at Ocean Beach last night. He asked me to come out there because he was in a lot of trouble and thought maybe I could help him. I think somebody followed me to him and killed him."

"Jesus. Who was it?"

"I don't know. I'm going to find out."

"You're writing a story about it?"

"No. Listen, this, uh, Carl. He seems solid, I wasn't kidding."

She hunched forward infinitesimally. I doubt anyone else would have noticed it, that almost subliminal shift into her fighting posture.

"Lottie, I didn't come down here to start trouble, really."

"That's because you're feeling sorry for yourself," she said. She walked over to her desk, one of those old roll-tops with a million pigeonholes and little drawers, and got a cigarette and lit it. "I don't need this, you know?"

"I just wanted to make sure you had your money, to do something right."

"*And* to get a little sympathy . . ." She paused but I knew what it was on the tip of her tongue to say. "And a little mothering for being a good boy," or something like that. To which I would have answered, "For God's sake, don't analyze me," and then we would have been off to the races. But she didn't finish the thought, so instead I smiled and told her, "It hurts to bite your tongue."

For the first time since I had come there our eyes engaged. "I was awfully angry at you for a long time, Ben. I didn't want to see you, you know? I'm getting over that, it's getting clearer to me that I played my role in it too. But I'm not there yet." She heaved a great sigh. "You want a cup of coffee or something?"

"Thanks, but I'm out of here in a minute."

"You sure? It's no trouble."

I shook my head.

"You know what I don't understand?"

"No, what?"

"Why me?" She raised her dark eyebrows questioningly.

"It's funny, that's the same thing I asked Yollo when he came to me. He was in trouble because the police suspected him of another killing. He said, 'Who else can I go to? I can't very well go to the cops.' "

"I don't get it," Lottie said.

"Nobody else to go to."

"Listen, you big dumb galoot, get your ass out of here." But she smiled when she said it. "Knowing you, you probably just climbed out of bed with some twenty-year-old and felt guilty."

"Yeah, well." I would be meeting Judy Shugart at Tosca's in a couple of hours. "I'm sorry it took so long to get your money. And grateful for what you said, you know, about being less angry. Tell Carl so long, okay?"

"I'll tell him."

I brushed her cheek with my knuckles and left, pulling the door shut behind me. I heard her throw the chain.

Instead of heading directly back to the city I stopped at a filling station and looked in the Yellow Pages. Cole Air Carriers was listed in Burlingame, just a few miles down the road. It would suit me just fine if Jerry Cole had been mixed up in Shugart's murder, and Aretha had said his business was located down this way. I thought I'd have a look around—there was still plenty of time before I had to meet Judy. I had the peaceful feeling you get when you had done something right for a change. I switched on the radio and the Giants were at bat in the bottom of the ninth, still trailing 4–2, but they had two runners on base and a big young first baseman named Mike Ivie was coming up to pinch-hit.

"Here's the pitch," Lon Simmons said, and there was the satisfying crack of bat striking ball. "Away back, away back. Tell it goodbye. A home run, the Giants win 5–4 . . ." An omen?

The sky was a deep hazy purple as I drove up the service road that led to the airfield. Above the ridge to the west there was a smudge of burnt orange on the horizon. Beyond the hills, out of sight, the sun was sliding into the Pacific. There probably wouldn't be anybody about at this hour, but even if there was, a taxi showing up at an airfield shouldn't arouse any suspicions. The airfield itself was nothing more than a single runway the length of an elliptical meadow with limp, conical orange flags lining the strip. The only building was a ramshackle cottage with neglected whitewash. Beside it were three red fuel pumps. Some small planes were standing south of the terminal. I thought of hooting the horn just in case somebody was home but I didn't want to get carried away with this disguise stuff. There was a light on inside the shack. I stopped the cab and approached quietly, pressing my face against a window and craning to see through a space between two slats in the grimy venetian blinds.

Inside a man was standing over a table zipping up a plump traveling bag. On the table were a bottle of vodka and two water tumblers. An ashtray full of butts had a cigarette still burning in it, but the cigarette wasn't facing the man with the flight bag, it was balanced on the lip of the ashtray across from him. In the time it took my fine investigator's mind to deduce that there had recently been two people about, the missing party introduced himself to me.

"What the fuck are you looking for, asshole?" The voice came from just behind me. I turned. He was wiry thin, maybe six feet tall, with shaggy hair. Faded tight fitting jeans, a purple teeshirt, some sort of amulet worn on a gold chain. He looked like a rock-'n'-roll musician, with a greyhound body probably kept lean by a diet of speed or coke. I barely took all that in, though, because I was transfixed by the gun in his hand that was pointing at my belly. My stomach muscles contracted involuntarily and the nape of my neck and my hands prickled with an ageless reflex that lifted the hair of an animal and made it look bigger, more dangerous, tougher to chew.

"I asked what the fuck you're doing here?"

"What's the gun for? You the fella who called for a taxi?" I figured that some sort of white-cabbie's-Stepin-Fetchit routine was my best hope of extricating myself.

"Nobody called for no fuckin' taxi, shitface."

The other one came out of the terminal then. He was a man of about fifty with an expressionless, rockhard face and gray hair neatly brushed tight over his scalp, wearing a black Ultrasuede coat and a tie with a bar clasp. His face was as charitable as a bossman's on a Georgia chain gang.

"You the one wanted a taxi, mister?"

He didn't say a word, just looked toward the rock-'n'-roller with a silent question. The gun was still pointed at my midriff.

"Can't you put that gun away, man? It scares me half to death."

"Nobody called for no fuckin' taxi." The gun in his hand nodded briefly, as if to agree. I was pretty sure it was a .38, the same gun the clerk at the Exchange had told me would kill 'em dead.

"Listen, there's some mistake here. We got a call to

send a taxi down for somebody at eight o'clock. I'm sorry to be late but I got a little lost. I think they said it was a Mr. Cole who wanted the cab to go up to the city. You want me to raise my dispatcher on the radio? She'll tell you. I mean, I drove all the way down here.''

"Cole?'' said the rock-'n'-roller. He looked questioningly toward Stoneface. Stoneface looked stoically back at him; he still hadn't opened his mouth. Now he said, "Jerry say anything about a taxi?'' There was something wrong with his speech organs; his voice came out of one of those little voice boxes they can surgically implant in the throat. It warbled and grated like ratchets being turned in an echo chamber. My knees went spongy.

"You want me to call him?'' asked the rock-'n'-roller.

Stoneface shook his head. "Forget it,'' he said from within his throat. "A mistake,'' he told me.

"You mean I drove all the way down here for nothing? There's gonna be hell to pay when I get my hands on that goddamn dispatcher.''

"Move, you cunt,'' said the skinny guy with the gun. He stepped closer and shoved my shoulder hard. I stumbled and almost lost my balance. He laughed, a hyenalike gasp. I felt myself trembling now but not with fear. I wanted to hurt him.

Without a word I went back to the taxi and headed toward the main road. At the freeway cloverleaf I pulled into a truck stop and splashed water on my face. I let the hot water run over my wrists. I was looking into the mirror above the basin, but I was seeing their faces and hearing the horrible voice of the man without a larynx. After a moment I noticed mica glints of stubble flashing under the fluorescent light. I needed a shave again. I also needed to ask the fellows down at Cole Air Carriers a question, so I knew I would be seeing them again. The thought of it brought a wide hard smile to my face in the mirror, a smile that exposed long teeth. What I wanted to know was how they had put their hands on the leather flight bag I had last seen on the patio of Enrico's, clutched between Yollo Current's feet.

12

I had just enough time to stop back at my place and change out of the urban lumberjack clothes I wore in the taxi before meeting Judy Shugart. I put on my newest jeans, a gray linen shirt open at the collar, and a blue blazer that did not have brass buttons. Despite the beneficial attention of Vince's scissors my hair looked like it was trying to keep appointments in four places at once. I combed it, then hesitated over whether to take the comb with me to Tosca's. There was a vanity involved in a man caring enough about his appearance to carry a comb that I was reluctant to acknowledge to anybody else. I left the comb behind. It had been a long night already, but I felt as if it were just beginning.

Tosca's enveloped me in a world well removed from the damp, raw chill of the street. Beneath the stately rhythms of Caruso singing ''Una furtiva lagrima'' on the jukebox the nickel-plated brass espresso-maker hissed as Joseph forced steam through a spigot into a glass. The bar was dim, lit only by a big chandelier with tiny shades hanging near the back from an amber ceiling that was fading and water stained. On the wall across from the long, polished wood bar were very large, dark murals of Italy.

Joseph nodded in the direction of my favorite stool, which was unoccupied. It was in an especially dark corner just to the right of the double glass doors. I put my smokes and matches on the smooth worn bar top and sighed with relief as I lowered my weight onto the padded stool. Three or four of the red upholstered booths at the back were occupied, and perhaps half the stools along the bar. There was a murmur of barroom conversation. I thought I was on time, but Judy Shugart wasn't there.

Joseph had a ruddy face that succeeded in always looking happy without spilling over into jollity. He wore a short white jacket and a black tie against a white-on-white shirt.

"Through for the night?" he asked, when he put a cocktail napkin—one without a silly cartoon on it—in front of me.

"Just starting is more like it." I ordered a Chivas on the rocks with a water chaser and while he poured the drink I laid a twenty on the bar and took out a cigarette, waiting to light it until I had a sip of the Scotch inside me.

The clock above the door showed a quarter past eleven, bar time. San Francisco bars set their clocks ahead so they can clear out their customers and lock their doors by the 2 a.m. curfew. Humming along with Caruso, Joseph put my drink in front of me and scooped up the twenty, returning with my change. I pushed a couple of singles out of the pile toward him—tipping a bartender when he brings the first round doesn't hurt the service you get from there on in—and left the rest on the bar. Every familiar step in this ritual warmed me and removed me further from the rock-'n'-roller and Stoneface. Once a long time ago I had to tell a man that his lover was dead. He stood as still as a man can stand and then he took a broom and began to sweep his kitchen floor, impressing me with the power of the mundane to express and assuage anguish. Ritual, as popes and generals both knew, had the power to create deep loyalties.

"What time is it really?" I asked Joseph.

He looked at his watch. "Eleven-oh-five. Is your watch broken, Mr. Henry?" Joseph had a way of standing on the balls of his feet with his fists leaning lightly against the inner edge of the bar.

"Don't own one."

"Why's that?"

"One day I got tired of checking on what time it was even when I already knew, so I took off my watch and dropped it in a drawer. Once you get rid of your watch you can't walk a block without finding out what time it is. There are clocks on buildings and clocks in stores, the radio and the television are always telling you what time it is, the world is crawling with reminders of the time."

"But what about when you're someplace with no clocks and you want to know what time it is?"

"There are no places with no clocks except elevators and public washrooms."

"Bars in airports. No clocks," Joseph said.

"Gotta be. I mean, that's the one place where everybody has *got* to know what time it is."

"Uh-uh. I used to work at the bar out at the airport and there was no clock. You know why? Because if the clock's wrong and somebody misses their flight they can sue you. Think about *that*, you don't think the world is crazy."

After a while I saw her hurrying across Columbus, moving more gracefully in her high-heeled slippers than most women can in sneakers, dodging traffic with long strides that never broke into a run, fast but contained. She wore a man's white shirt that was way too big for her and ballooned over a pair of very tight designer jeans, and she was tucking an errant wisp of hair behind her ear, even as she legged it through the moving traffic against the light. She came through the swinging glass door with her composure as bright and certain as neon.

"Oh, God, I'm sorry, I'm late again," she said when she saw me. She climbed on the stool next to mine. "You have a drink. I wanted to buy you a drink."

Joseph was already standing in front of her, smiling. Along the bar men were turning away from their dates and their wives to look toward her. She was the kind of woman who walked into a room and every man in it suddenly had secrets. "Do you have any iced Stolichnaya?" she asked him.

"Pardon, ma'am?"

"Russian vodka, do you keep it frozen?"

"No, ma'am, we don't."

"It doesn't matter. A Smirnoff on the rocks." She dug into a large canvas bag with leather straps—it looked like a carpenter's bag—and came out with a plump blue packet of Gauloises and a chunky box of wood matches. Perfect attention to every detail of her style.

"Well," I said. I was wary but no longer angry with her. A man would have to be far less lonely than I was to stay angry at a creature so beautifully alive as she was. Joseph put her drink down and held a lighter to her cigarette. She went into her bag again, rummaging for money, but Joseph had already taken it out of my pile of bills and silver. I listened to the distinctive sounds made by the contents of a woman's handbag, which made music the way dice did clicking across a table.

"I'm buying the next one," she said and took a sip of her drink. When she put the glass down there was a lipstick impression on it. "You look a lot more like yourself dressed like this," she said. "C'mon, don't look so suspicious. I know, you're telling yourself that this is a crazy, untrustworthy dame, but listen, Henry, a girl is entitled to more than one chance when she's as special as I am. That's it, Henry, that's what I like to see, a teensy bitsy little smile. I told you, I'm just a scatterbrain whose father's been murdered, and whose fiancé . . . well, forget it, *that* isn't who you want to hear about."

"Jer-baby? What about Jer-baby?"

"Do you really want to hear all of this?" Her white blouse was open several buttons deep at her neck to reveal a generous share of smooth, tight skin.

"That's why I'm here."

"Is it? He's acting strange—well, no, that's not really it. He's acting suspicious. I mean I'm suspicious. Of him."

"Suspicious of what?"

"God, I shouldn't be talking like this, out of school. I mean, I hardly know you and you're a reporter and God knows I know what that means, and why too. You don't have to justify it to me, Henry, I bought the party line from Harry hook, line and stinker. Look, I trust you. Oh, Christ, what a cliché. I'm making a mess of this, right? C'mon, Henry, give me a hand. Don't just sit there like some god waiting to be appeased.''

"You know the Bob Dylan song that goes 'Something's going on here and you don't know what it is, do you, Mr. Jones?' That's who I feel like, Mr. Jones. *What* do you suspect Jerry of?''

"Killing Harry. It's not that I have any proof or anything. Do you, Mr. Jones?''

"Do I have any proof, or do I know what's going on here?''

"You know the first time I heard Bob Dylan I was fifteen,'' she said. "There was a real greaser, outlaw type in my high school, all the girls in my set just looked down their noses at him. But he had a crush on me. He used to leave poems in my locker, I mean none of the boys *I* knew wrote poems, and here was this guy who was supposed to be some kind of Neanderthal, and *he* wrote poems. Finally one day he came up to me when nobody else was around, he was afraid of being teased if anybody saw him, and he asked me to go for a ride on his motorcycle. I said no, I mean girls like me didn't go out with guys like him, but then I thought about it some more and the next time I saw him I told him I would, okay. We rode for a long time, really fast, and then he took me back to his place— he was eighteen and he was the first boy I ever knew who didn't live with his parents. We smoked a joint and he put on a Bob Dylan record. It was the one with the song about the sad-eyed lady of the lowlands. I was completely fascinated with him by that time. We saw each other for the rest of the school year and all summer but then he dropped me. I don't blame him, either. I still made fun of him to my friends, maybe he sensed that. I was so damn young and I didn't know anything. I wouldn't go to bed with him, either.''

Her glass was empty and I waved for Joseph to bring another round. This time I lit her cigarette.

"Yollo's been murdered," I told her.

"The coke dealer?" A jolt of fear appeared in her lustrous blue eyes and passed as quietly as a single dash of Morse code.

"Yeah."

"Why does everybody keep bringing him up? What's he got to do with this? Who killed him?"

"Whoever killed your father, I'd guess. If you want me to trust you, you should stop lying. You knew Yollo, didn't you?"

"I didn't know him, but I can see why you think I did." She frowned.

"You even lied to me about which taxi company you called that night," I told her. "Now that's a degree of overkill that I find charmingly American, actually."

"Okay, I deserved that too. When are we even, Jones? Not until I tell you about it, right? Jerry was involved in a coke deal with this Yollo, I never did meet him. I'm telling you the truth now. I don't deal, I don't need to, there are always men ready to give me cocaine if I want it, all I want. Jerry asked me to take the delivery from Yollo. I don't know why he did, but he said he had his reasons. Anyway it didn't seem like any big deal besides being a little dangeroso, and I like that. Yollo was supposed to come by at eleven-thirty but I don't know if he did or didn't, I don't know if he was there at all, I was late like I always am. When Jerry came I told him Yollo hadn't shown up, not that I was late. I knew how disappointed Jerry would be. He got real angry about it and it frightened me, he's a violent guy. When he went away I called a taxi. I wanted to get out of there, something had really gone wrong and it was my fault. I felt like such a dumb girl again. But Jerry came back, he wasn't angry at me anymore, he's like that and so am I, quick to get hot and quick to cool off. He said we should go have a drink. So we went to Cafe Royale and we didn't talk about it. I don't know why he didn't want to, but I didn't because I didn't want to get him angry again. That's what *really* happened. Do you believe me now, Mr. Jones?"

I wasn't sure, desire and doubt were staging a tug-of-war. Whatever was going on in the big house on Jackson Street that night I could believe Judy Shugart had wanted to get out of there in a hurry. Even under the most placid circumstances the girl was hardly a homebody. "You didn't know your father was dead?"

She shook her head. "I have my own apartment with a private entrance around the side of the house. I didn't go into Harry's part of the house until the police took us in there later on."

"Do you know a couple of guys, one's skinny and wears cowboy boots and necklaces and the other one's got no larynx, he talks through a box in his throat?"

"Frimmer," she said, "the one with the throat, he makes me want to wet my pants. They work for Jerry. The other one is Pendleton, Randy Pendleton. How did I get involved with all of this? If you really want to know, I'm through with Jerry but I haven't told him. I'm afraid of him. I'm scared, Jones. Are you gonna be my knight-errant?"

"Me? I can barely find my way across the street these days."

"How come you don't write for *The Courier* anymore?"

"The publisher fired me."

"Dick Thiesmann?"

"You know him?"

"Well, I've met him around. He's pretty arrogant, isn't he?"

"He had one of his lackeys fire me. He told me I was careless and reckless."

"You are reckless. That's why I'm keeping an eye on you."

"For who?"

"For myself. I was talking to a girl friend about you, and you know what she said? 'Not another *poor* one, Judy.' I can't help it, I've got a thing about poor, reckless guys."

"Thiesmann doesn't know it, but I'm going to make him regret it."

"Are you? Do you mean it?"

"As much as I've ever meant anything."

"Here's to it." She lifted her glass to mine. After we drank she held her glass toward Joseph to indicate we were ready for more drinks.

"You liked being a reporter, huh? How'd you get into the ink-stained-wretch racket?"

"I used to work for an antipoverty agency back East, when it was still a new thing, Lyndon Johnson and the war on poverty. I was shiny bright, I could see my virtue reflected in the shine on my cordovan wingtips. Working in the ghetto in Baltimore educated me. I could handle the despair all right, when I saw how really enduring those people with no hope were. I went from feeling charitable—which was just a form of feeling superior—to feeling humble. It took about a year. Humble and angry. What I was angry about, mostly, was the head of the agency, a very bright, very smooth, very sincere sounding black guy named Clarence Perkins. I finally caught on that Perks wasn't so much interested in eradicating poverty as he was in getting elected to Congress. He had dozens of young guys and gals like me on the federal payroll, and our real job was to bring the name of Clarence Perkins into every house in the ghetto.

"What brought it to a head for me was the riot after Martin Luther King was shot, the summer of 1968. Everything was burning. I walked through the streets and the glass crunched under my shoes. There were little kids on the stoops, bawling, scared to death, and their parents were powerless to explain to them what was happening. Sirens, every once in a while a gunshot, the air so thick with smoke you could hardly breathe. People so mad with frustration they were destroying anything they could reach and all that was was the little bit they had. Charlie—it's been a long time since I said that, Charlie—Charlie even had insurance to turn a buck on their self-destruction. I ended up standing outside a market smoking a cigarette and up the street comes a guy who was very drunk, drunk all day, I guess, because when he got dressed he put on three shirts, all Ban-Lon, a green, a gold, and a grape. When this old guy in his three Ban-Lon shirts gets to the market he stops and peers inside, like he's surprised it's closed. He tries the door, but naturally it's locked. Then he notices a big hole in the plate glass where it's been smashed in. Very gingerly he steps through, avoiding the jagged edges of glass, and he gets himself a cart. It's dark in there, but there are some lights in the refrigerator cabinets and I can just make him out. Anyway, he starts wheeling his cart up and down the aisles, right past meats, expensive stuff, even past the wine and beer. He's looking for something, he's *shopping*. Up one aisle, down the next, until he finds it. He reaches out and takes a box and puts it in his shopping cart and wheels it down toward the checkout counters. Finally I can see what's in the cart, it's a box of Cap'n Crunch. Man needs his breakfast, riot or no riot. He waits by a register but finally he comes to understand nobody's there. What can he do? He shrugs, takes his box of cereal in both hands, but just as he's stepping back through the window two prowl cars whip around the corner. One of 'em hits the siren just once, it sounds like a calf being slaughtered, and they shine a high-intensity beam right in his face. He puts a hand up to shield his eyes, keeping a solid grip on the Cap'n Crunch, and starts on his way home. Whatever these honky cops want, it's got nothing to do with him. Four cops grab ahold of him.

" 'You're under arrest,' a cop says.

" 'Me? What for?' The guy's genuinely baffled.

" 'Don't jiveass me, you're a thief.' Another cop grabs the Cap'n Crunch. Evidence.

" 'Me?' says the guy in the three Ban-Lon shirts. 'Me? I never stole nothing in my life.'

"The cop in charge says, 'Take him away,' and shoves him into a prowl car.

"Anyway, I quit a little while after that and got a job at the paper. It seemed to me I could do more by writing stories like that than by helping Perks become a congressman."

"Did it work out?" she asked.

"Well, I became a reporter, Perks got elected the next year, and I never wrote the story of the man in the three Ban-Lon shirts. The things you want to do the most are the hardest to do."

"Not always," she said and leaned forward, balancing herself by resting a hand on my knee, to kiss me. She smelled and tasted wonderful, of clean skin and vodka and temptation.

"Not in public." I was embarrassed.

"You love to show off, don't you, Mr. Jones?"

I had to admit I was happier than I would have been if she hadn't kissed me. "I'm going to call you a cab, a Luxor with one of those nice old men driving it, and send you home."

"Home," she said, "isn't what I want."

"Oh."

"Oh." She did a pretty fair imitation.

"There's a little concave place in your throat that palpitates when you're lying."

"Is it palpitating now?" I could feel her warm breath on my face. "Home," she said again, "isn't what I want."

"No, it isn't palpitating." I went to the pay phone anyway.

13

Patience was a virtue I greatly admired because I had so little of it myself. As I began my fourth hour of sitting in my cab just up the block from Ricky Thiesmann's flat I was not enjoying myself. Leaning on Ricky because he was vulnerable was not something I liked to do, but I thought he could probably shed some light on what had gone on the night Harry Shugart was murdered, and I needed more facts.

I wasn't concerned that a neighbor might become suspicious of my sitting there so long and call the cops. A taxi is a perfect cover for surveillance. People are accustomed to taxis waiting at the curb: how many songs were there about taxis waiting for lovelorn departures? It would be a good cover for a burglar casing a house too, and I knew drivers who picked up passengers only incidentally, using their cabs to deal dope, collect betting slips, and in the case of one woman driver, to sell pleasure in the back seat. I wonder if she kept the meter running. It was the kind of question to spark a debate of almost theological dimensions among drivers.

The minutes ticked tediously by. Ricky, or somebody, was home in the flat, which was a white Victorian with a deep red bougainvillea trellised around the stairs and the oak front door. At dusk the lights had been turned on in the long, narrow bay window at the front, and through the flocked curtains I could see the shadows of house plants. Nobody had gone in or come out.

From time to time I could catch Judy Shugart's scent, or the memory of it. I wished I understood better what I wanted from her, what she wanted from me. Like the olfactory memory of her scent, the question of what I wanted was tantalizing because it was so delicate and ephemeral, eluding my grasp each time I thought I almost had it. I decided to stretch my legs.

I had reached the corner, walking slowly with my hands jammed into my pockets, and turned back up the tree-lined, leafy nighttime street when Ricky came out of his house and down the porch steps. Now here was an instance of classic detection, a textbook example. You spend half the night lurking behind the wheel of your taxi setting a trap in which to catch somebody unawares, and then you get caught with your flat feet on the pavement about to encounter your man face to face, just the way you didn't want to. As he went by me, walking toward Fillmore Street, I bent down and pretended to tie my shoelace. When he had almost reached the corner I sprinted to the cab and jumped in and drove after him.

O Great God of Undeserved Good Fortune, your humble servant thanks you: Ricky was halfway down Fillmore toward Washington Street with his hand raised to flag a taxi.

"How are you tonight?" he asked when he got in. He had fine, delicate features. His short hair and his dark mustache were both neatly trimmed. He was wearing pleated slacks, penny loafers, and a white sweater with an alligator above his heart. He carried a tan windbreaker.

"Don't ask. Where to?"

"We need to go to Nineteenth and Sanchez and pick somebody up and then we're going on," he said.

I headed north, deeper into Pacific Heights and toward the Golden Gate Bridge.

"No, this is the wrong way. Don't you know how to get to Nineteenth and Sanchez?" He was annoyed.

"I know, Ricky. We're just going to take a little ride."

"Who the hell are you?" His voice was rising angrily. "Where do you think you're taking me?"

I accelerated and started rolling through the stop signs as we headed downhill toward the dark water of the Bay, the lights of Alcatraz and Tiburon glowing softly. I was praying that there was no cop around and that Ricky didn't have the nerve to bail out of a fast-moving vehicle on a steep hill.

"Let me out of here, goddamnit."

"I'm a spook, Ricky. I want to have a little chat with you."

"You're fucking crazy."

"I'm with DEA," I said, catching his eye in the rear-view mirror.

"The Drug Something-or-other?"

"Drug Enforcement Administration." I flashed my phony ID.

"That doesn't give you the right to goddamn kidnap me. I want to get out right this minute."

He sounded a little too confident to suit me, more angry than scared.

"Ricky," I said, "we know all about what happened up at Mr. Shugart's house. The cocaine, the gun, your father. I think you'll find it's in your best interest to talk with us. Strictly on a confidential basis."

"Oh, God." It was a moan. "Oh, Jesus God, let me out of here." That was better.

I timed it just right, hitting the green light at Lombard Street, and swung out toward the bridge, but I had to run the last red light on Richardson Drive. In a flash we were on the span crossing to Marin County. There was a crew doing road work but there were two lanes open going north and I was able to move at a pretty good clip, passing Leaper's Rail and wondering fleetingly, as I did every time I drove by, why virtually all the six hundred suicides who had gone over had chosen to face the city rather than the open sea.

The tunnel leading to the recreation preserve is a long, narrow tube with traffic moving through it only one way at a time. I hurtled through between ill-lit, aged walls that pressed in close on both sides. About halfway through he said, "What cocaine?"

I didn't answer. On a stretch of empty road a half-mile beyond the tunnel I pulled to the side and shut off the motor. "Tell me about it, Ricky." I turned halfway around to face him. We were disembodied by the dark and solitary nature of the spot.

"I don't know anything about cocaine. I don't know what you're talking about." He would have liked to be angry but lacked the nerve.

"Ricky, I could shake you down right now and we both know I'd find your poppers and probably some grass too. The bust wouldn't stand up in court, we both know that too. But I'll bet that part of it worries you less than how your father would react."

"Fuck you."

I waited.

"What do you want to know?"

"Let's start with you and Mr. Shugart."

He began to sniffle. "Harry," he said. "Harry."

"How did your father find out about it, Ricky?"

"He—he found Harry's letters. I never thought he'd do that. I mean, he always respected my privacy before. Somebody must have told him something because when I came home he was waiting with the letters. All around on the floor. It was a mess. He had a gun. Oh, God."

"I understand."

"No, you don't. You don't understand at all. He didn't really mean it. He was just so upset he was saying things he didn't mean. He didn't really mean it."

"When he said he was going to kill Harry?"

That produced sobs. He took out a handkerchief and blew his nose. "Yes, no. He said a lot of things. He was certain Harry had seduced me. And—and—you know, I couldn't tell him . . . I mean I just told him he was wrong, so wrong. But he wouldn't, you know, he didn't even hear me. He was trembling. I thought the gun was going to go off right there. It was like he really didn't hear what I was

saying. 'The bastard's going to pay for doing this to me.'
He was saying it over and over in a—I don't know—a kind
of lifeless way. I felt like he didn't even really know I was
there. Well, *that* was nothing new.'' He laughed harshly.
''I mean, I couldn't help thinking how ironic it was, my
father avenging my honor, Mr. Cold and Upright. I—I
should have said to him, 'You, *you're* the bastard.' ''

''But you didn't.''

He shook his head.

''You did what he told you to do.''

He nodded. ''Yeah, yes. I—I didn't call Harry. I just
stayed put. Followed orders. 'Stay put!' And—and I'll
never forgive myself, not if I live to be a hundred. Who
would care anyway? I could kill myself tomorrow and
n-nobody would give a fuck anyway.''

''What happened after that, Ricky?''

''Well, I stayed put until he came back again. I just sat
there in the rocker like a zombie or something waiting to
see what was going to happen to me. Then he was there.
He looked even worse than before he left, he looked as
frightened as I was. And I thought, oh, God, he did it, he
really did it. But he said, 'I want you to believe this. Harry
is dead, I found him dead. I never intended to shoot him.
I don't know what I was planning except that I was going
to make him regret what he did to you, Richard.' Harry
didn't *do* anything except to love me. Oh, Christ, oh, fucking Christ, what a mess.''

''Did you believe him, Ricky?''

''No—yes. I don't know. Yes. I did.''

''Why?''

''You don't know my father. If you did you'd believe
him too. I mean, he has too much self-control, he gets
colder when he's angry. The Iceman Cometh, that's one
of my little jokes about how I was born altogether. And—
and he told me he didn't kill Harry. Telling the truth is a
very big thing with him.''

''So you believed him?''

''I really didn't care that much. I mean, Harry was dead.
Dead dead dead dead dead.'' He began to cry again.

"What happened then, Ricky?"

"Well, he took me home, back to his house I mean, and I took a couple of Valium." He looked sharply at me. "I have a prescription. From my shrink."

I nodded.

"Valium and a drink. And don't tell me they don't mix, they're a perfect mix for what I wanted, oblivion, bye-bye land."

"What about your father?"

"Oh, he made some phone calls. That's how he always deals with a crisis. I take Valium and he makes phone calls."

"Who did he call, do you know?"

"His lawyer. And that cop, I suppose."

"Which cop was that?"

"The great big black plainclothes detective, I don't know his name. He came by just when I was nodding out and they talked."

Pressix. Pressix. "I see."

"But I don't know anything about cocaine, I really don't."

"I believe you, Ricky. I'll drive you back now." I wasn't proud of what I had done and we didn't talk, not even when I let him out.

By the time I pulled into Adler Alley it was quite late. I hadn't even shut off the motor when my windscreen exploded in my face, showering me with glass. There was a car across the far lip of the alley on Grant and when it took off I went after it. I chased it across Broadway past the sailors and the sellers and the strip joints. Big Al's with its neon image of the machine-gun-toting hoodlum made an ironic dig at the edge of my awareness. The wind rushing through the shot-out window plastered me to the seat. I was brushing glass off my eyebrows and out of my hair.

I almost lost control on the hairpin curve of the bridge approach but barely hung on. I was a pretty good distance behind them and not gaining. We were both whipping around other cars, leaving a trail of outraged honking horns behind us. Not just horns, a siren. I turned for a quick look, my neck being snapped almost 180 degrees by the force of the wind, and saw flashing red and yellow lights.

As they entered the tunnel at midspan I got a clearer look at their car, a gray station wagon with two men in it. On the rear bumper was a sticker. It said, "Pilots Stay Up Longer."

14

I didn't hit the sack until the sky was turning a paler shade of gray and pigeons were twittering beneath the eaves. First there was a livid state cop to deal with and then the boss of Checker Cab Company, who got out of his bed and came down to the yard to question me about what had happened. I told them both the simple truth, the taxi had been shot at by a couple of Chinese kids in a red Pontiac Firebird. No, I had never seen them before. No, I had no idea why anybody would shoot at me. Wasn't that just the way Chinese kids in red Firebirds had fun these days? No, I would never chase anybody again at ninety miles an hour across the Bay Bridge. No, no, no. Thank you very much, officer. Thank you, Mr. Lemon, I agree, a week off might be a good idea. Thank you, thank you, one and all. And to all a good night.

The goddamn telephone woke me again. I would have to start unplugging it so it wouldn't be waking me up first thing every afternoon. I picked it up on the fourth ring but whoever was on the other end hung up when they heard my voice.

"May you rot in a hot tub," I said to the dead line. "May they drink an intelligent little white wine at your funeral." As long as I had the phone in my hand I dialed the service.

"Oh, hello, Be-en," Peter said. I never failed to be

impressed by how Peter managed to extract two syllables from my name. "I have a message for you that is disturbing me, Ben."

"I paid her, Peter, honest to God."

"Oh, that was the right thing to do, Ben. I am very glad to hear that. You have no idea—"

I interrupted. "For God's sake, Peter, what's the message?"

There was a long, hurt pause.

"Hey, I'm sorry, Peter. Got a rotten hangover."

"Have you tried a raw egg yolk in V8 juice with Tabasco sauce, Ben? Magic."

Forty bucks. The answering service cost me forty bucks a month. Hangover remedies I'm getting for my forty bucks. "Sounds yummy, Peter. What did Lottie say?"

"Lottie? Oh, she has not called, Ben. You were expecting her?"

"I thought . . . never mind. What's the disturbing message?"

"I will read it to you exactly, Ben. I wrote it down every word for word the way the man said it exactly. Ready? Here goes. 'Your gun and registration is ready.' Why does everybody in America want to own a gun, Ben?"

"It's not for me, Peter. It's a present for somebody who lives up in the Sierras and hunts game birds."

"You would not shoot a person, would you, Ben?"

I thought of the rock-'n'-roller who had shoved me, of Jer-baby and Thiesmann. I even thought of a kid who used to pick on me in the third grade. "No, Peter, never."

"I am so relieved to hear that, you have no idea. The Northern California Gun Control Society, Ben, has a tape that is very informative."

"I'll give it a listen. I want to run out now and get some V8 and eggs. Is that the only message?"

"Oh, no. There are others, Ben. Miss Judy Shugart called. She would like to hear from you. And a Mr. Nellie called also. He says he wants to discuss the shape of the table. Are you redecorating, Ben?"

I looked around at my bits and sticks of furniture. "No,

Peter, not yet. Mr. Nellie? Oh, Nellie Flynn, the shape of the table.'' Nellie must have some information he wanted to trade. ''Thanks, Peter, I'm all set now.''

''Have a nice, Ben.''

I was doubtful of the likelihood of that, but it seemed worth the old college try. In the shower I sang the two lines each I knew of ''On Wisconsin'' and ''Roar Lion Roar.'' The hot shower helped me feel human again, and the shave helped too. There is a bracing dispute in certain quarters over whether a shave or a shower is the more restorative ablution. I hold with the shower, but of course it depends on the sufficiency of the heated-water pressure. It was while I was shaving that I remembered what Ricky had told me about Franklin Delano Roosevelt Pressix visiting Thiesmann on the night Shugart was murdered. The razor kept moving but momentarily I forgot all about it and nicked myself. I stuck a piece of tissue paper on the cut to serve as a reminder that Pressix and I might be at cross-purposes, and that I had to figure out what to do about it.

I slipped into the pants of a light brown herringbone suit and a short sleeve white shirt before I poured the water from the boiling kettle through the ground coffee. The coffee was okay but I preferred Peet's of Berkeley. The Berkeleyites were an exotic breed with their Earth Shoes and book bags: pedestrians crossed in front of moving cars with self-righteous grins, and people on bicycles seemed to think they were making a political statement. Maybe I would drive over to Berkeley, buy some coffee, go book shopping at Moe's. With me in my Hickey-Freeman suit and my favorite tie—a rich brown silk with a treble clef symbol—and hard shoes with a spit shine, clean shaven and well shorn, everybody in Berkeley would take me for an alien. My mood was almost festive. Big John Lemon didn't know what a favor he was doing when he suspended me from driving the taxi for a week. When I got back from Berkeley I could pick up the gun and see Judy Shugart. Maybe I would skip Berkeley altogether and proceed directly to Judy. And the gun. The two seemed a good fit.

A quiet knock at the door interrupted this interesting train of thought.

"Nobody here but us chickens," I shouted.

"Henry?"

"Is that you, Colonel Sanders?"

"We want to talk to you, Henry." It was a male voice, unfamiliar.

"Easy, Spike," I said. "Easy, boy. Sit. Sit ready, Spike. That's a boy. Sit ready now." I went to the door and opened it a crack. There were two of them both nicely dressed in quiet suits. "What?" I said.

"Mr. Wallach sent us, Henry. You know Mr. Wallach?"

"No." I put one hand behind me out of sight at waist level. "Easy, Spike."

"Mr. Wallach knows you," said the one who did the talking. "He also knew Mr. Current. Mr. Current had something of Mr. Wallach's that he is anxious to have back. Do you think we could come in and discuss this thing like gentlemen?"

"I don't have what you're looking for."

"Mr. Wallach thought maybe you were looking for it, the way he is. He thought if you knew its whereabouts maybe Beans here and me could help. You see?"

I considered asking them if they would wait outside while I ran down to the Gun Exchange and picked up my new weapon. Instead I said, "Come on in." I walked back to the stove and left them to push open the door while I poured myself a cup of courage.

"That's very good, I like that," said the one who did the talking, once they were inside. He was about fifty years old, stocky, and half a head shorter than me with washed out eyes behind thick glasses with wide black frames.

"Graffeo's, light roast."

"I mean the dog bit."

"Oh, yeah, old family trick. You want some coffee?"

"Why not?" He seemed to speak for his sidekick, who was shorter than he was and broader, with wide sloping shoulders and a bullet head. He looked like he could bend steel bars. All his features were small: tiny eyes, a pug nose, small cauliflower ears. He smiled at me as if we shared a private joke.

"Help yourselves."

I leaned against the counter and inhaled the rich steam rising off my coffee. They both poured themselves coffee and sat down at the table. They resembled each other in being indistinct. Quiet, ordinary faces, quiet, ordinary suits. Black lace-up shoes. I was willing to wager they were both wearing guns under their jackets. They looked like accountants, very dangerous accountants.

"Wait a second," I said. "Are you guys feds?"

"I already told you we're from Mr. Wallach."

"Yeah, but you look like feds."

"What should we look like?"

"I don't know, Rocco and Tony maybe."

He smiled without any mirth. The flesh of his neck sagged. "My name is Paul Wagner. Beans's name you were already given." Beans nodded, still smiling his conspiratorial smile. "Mr. Wallach heard you had a little trouble with some people. These are people who have caused him trouble too. Very troublesome people. Together we might be able to get what we want from these people, he thought."

"Depends."

"Depends on what?"

"On what we both want."

"Mr. Wallach thought you wanted a story for your newspaper."

"If I wanted a story for the newspaper I couldn't accept Mr. Wallach's help."

"You have lost me," Paul Wagner said.

"Never mind. No, I don't want a story for the newspaper." I thought about it. "I want the people who killed Yollo. For openers."

"He was a good friend of yours?"

"No."

"I see."

"Do you?"

He shrugged. "What does it matter? We want the same thing."

"The same people."

He shrugged again.

"Okay, yeah, I could probably help you recover what you're looking for. But if I do, how do I know that Mr. Wallach won't decide I'm disposable?"

"If that was the way Mr. Wallach was thinking, Henry, do you suppose we'd all be sitting around here sipping coffee like gentlemen?"

"What do you have in mind?"

"You know where these people are?"

"I have a pretty good idea."

"And what we are looking for?"

I nodded.

"Then what we will do is go there and take back what belongs to Mr. Wallach."

"The three of us?"

"Absolutely."

"I don't want any of what Mr. Wallach lost," I said. "I don't want any money. Or a story either."

"What are you after then?"

"I want Mr. Wallach's cooperation on a matter of personal importance to me. I want to sit down with Mr. Wallach and ask for his help on this other matter."

"I will talk to Mr. Wallach and get you his assurance, that should be no problem. Maybe tonight will be a good time to take care of our mutual business."

"With the assurance."

They both stood up and went to the door. The talker reached into a pocket and extracted a business card from a case. "Here. You can reach me here." The card said Wallach Associates, in raised letters. In the lower lefthand corner was his name, Paul Wagner, and a phone number. I listened to their footsteps all the way down, strumming the card with my thumb until the bell on the outside door jingled.

"Easy, Spike," I said.

15

I didn't know what to do next so I went downstairs and browsed through the bookstore. At the cash register Joel Petry, who managed the store, seemed surprised by the book I'd picked.

"Iris Murdoch?" he said. "You like her, huh?"

"I don't know. A friend said she was good." Buddy liked her novels.

"Well, maybe you'll like Jessica Gage too." He pointed toward a poster that said Jessica Gage, the author of *Ordinary Losses*, would be signing copies there on Sunday.

Ordinary losses. It put me in mind of Buddy and Yollo and Lottie, of how the entire business of living seemed sometimes to be measured in increments of attrition. Two men I didn't much like, Yollo and Harry Shugart, had died violently and because of that my life was turned inside out. I met a woman who excited me, people shot at me, I bought a gun, but most important of all I felt alive again because I was looking for answers to questions that were supposed to be none of my business.

"It's a good title."

"You should stop by on Sunday."

As I stepped outside I saw a bottle-green Plymouth sedan in the bus zone at my front door with the young plainclothes cop who was Pressix's new partner sitting at the wheel, so I ducked back inside and waited. A moment later Pressix came out of my building and they drove away. It was supposed to have worked the other way, but seeing Pressix reminded me of the tissue paper stuck to my chin and I tore it away, reopening the cut, which began to bleed.

The Walther was waiting for me at the Gun Exchange, looking more beautiful than lethal in its box. I hefted it and rubbed it and sighted along its barrel, beginning to understand what the fellow had meant when he asked me if I wanted a friend.

"A beauty, isn't it?" he said as I handled it.

He showed me again how to load and unload the clip and explained that I wasn't allowed to have the weapon on my person; the license permitted me to keep the gun in my home only. I took my package and strolled up Market Street, eyeing the people passing by from a perspective that had been subtly altered by the weapon under my arm. There was a thrilling edge in the possession of a gun on the street. I felt in more danger than I had before but also confident of handling it. The gun had the hyperbolic power of whiskey without any loss of sobriety. I carried my package to a pay phone and put it down on the shelf. Her number was busy so I tried Nellie Flynn, keeping a wary eye on whether anybody was approaching me, and a hand on the gun.

Somebody at the city desk growled, "He's at the cop shack." It was a number I knew as well as if it were my own, which it had been.

"Flynn."

"Yo, Nellie. Ben Henry."

"What the fuck do you think you're doing?"

"Who wants to know?"

"Now what the tired fuck does that mean?"

"It means you, or *The Courier*?" Nellie had been good, one of the best, until too many spiked or swallowed stories and whiskey chasers to wash away the bad taste had reduced him to going through the motions and no more than that, a kind of salaried retirement that never slipped into slipshod work of a kind that would have been undignified. He filed the necessary stories and spent the rest of his time in cop bars, but when I had started my series about the cops he had maintained a studied cynicism about my naïveté in public and fed me leads when nobody was looking. Maybe he thought I would inflict some wounds that he would have liked to himself.

"Thiesmann wants your balls on a platter. Can you top this one—Mazer's got me working on figuring out what you're up to."

"They think I'm writing something?"

"They think you're guilty of kidnapping, assault with intent to do great bodily harm, impersonating a law enforcement officer—let's see, there's more, I'm just looking through my notes here . . ."

"Ricky's body ain't that great."

"You used to be straight."

"Did I? I don't remember."

"Remember Nellie at Christmas," he said, and hung up without saying goodbye. It was funny how under the right circumstances loathing could bring a man closer to doing the right thing than any of the cardinal virtues.

This time she answered on the first ring.

"You beckoned," I said.

"Oh, Jones. Did you get my card?"

"No. What card?"

"I mailed you a card. Are you busy? I've got something for you."

"What'd you have in mind?"

"Come by here. Around the side, to my place."

"How will I know if I found the right door?"

"Easy."

"I'll be an hour."

"I'll manage." She laughed and hung up.

A Chinese swabber in a bloody white smock was dumping a bucket of fish entrails into the red dumpster in Adler Alley when I pulled in after first circling the block to make sure that Pressix wasn't waiting for me. I wasn't ready to talk with Pressix yet. The mail had been delivered. The telephone company had written to remind me of how eagerly they awaited my payment. And there was a postcard with a picture of a glistening red apple and a message on the back that said, "On the shelf." It was signed Judy.

I put the Walther, still in its box, on the top shelf of the wardrobe behind my baseball glove, with the box of clips and the holster beside it. I looked around carefully again before I left the building.

I was excited thinking about her on my way to see Judy Shugart. "Home," she had said, "isn't what I want." I had wanted to believe that, oh, how I wanted to believe her, and half did, but because she wrenched loose all the protective layers I had built up since I had left Lottie, I could not let go. I held back. She was too beautiful for me not to want to trust her, too beautiful to trust.

Instead of climbing the parapet steps to the Shugart residence I followed a flagstone path around the side of the house. The path was sheltered by tree-size lilac bushes with dainty pendulous blossoms. I didn't hear her approaching when I knocked so I was startled when the door opened inward. She peeped around the edge, her golden hair brushed out and hanging soft and loose. With no makeup on she looked very young and achingly lovely. She brought a lump to my throat. When she saw it was me her face lit up and she opened the door the rest of the way. She was barefoot, from her painted toes to her shocking blue eyes. So flawlessly beautiful.

As I stepped forward she threw herself into my arms and kissed me, our mouths opening. I hesitated.

"What's the matter, Jones? Is it too hot for you?" She was talking right into my ear, breathing warmly as she spoke.

"I don't know."

"Now, Jones, now. Don't say no again. I turn it on fast and I can turn it off just as fast."

My hands ran down over the taut skin of her back to where it curved and then flared at her hips. And then the floodgates burst and I hoisted her against me and we were on the floor, rolling together and gasping and laughing. I would have needed more than two hands to touch her soft, tight flesh in all the places and all the ways I wanted to.

She began to unbutton my shirt. I said, "In the afternoon." It was meant as a question but didn't come out that way.

Afterward she leaned against my shoulder with her hand resting warmly against my chest, and I breathed in the scent of her and held tight to the heat where our bodies touched. We did not talk but several times laughed out loud. I felt lighter, freer, more content than I thought possible. I kissed her, now in a tender, exploratory, less consumed way, but no less hungrily. What seemed a long time later she made us coffee, which she served in glass cups, and we sat together on a white rayon couch and smoked cigarettes.

She pulled my head down to hers and stared at me. Her eyes were dreamy. "I really like you, Jonesy. No kidding."

Past her shoulder was a closed door, the other side of the same door I had noticed in the room where we talked when I first came to Shugart's house. There was a key in the lock.

"That's the connecting door?"

"Uh-huh." She didn't turn to look at it.

"But you keep it locked on this side?"

"Harry understood I wanted my privacy."

"Why didn't you like him?"

"I blamed him for a lot of things, I guess. It doesn't matter now, does it? It really hasn't sunk in yet that I won't ever talk to him again. I mean, I think about him more than I did when he was alive. Do you know what I mean, that he's more alive in my thoughts?"

"My friend was murdered more than a year ago and I still talk to him sometimes."

"Then it doesn't sound weird to you that when I think of Harry now it's . . . what's the word—not sensual—tactile? As if I can touch him. Except for a peck on the cheek I don't think he touched me since I was fourteen or fifteen years old. I matured early. I was as big at fourteen as I am now, as developed. He seemed ashamed to touch me."

"What did he think of Jerry-baby?"

"He never said. I mean, Jerry wasn't the first man in my life."

"But you were engaged?"

"I suppose. He's a useful man. Will you help me, Jones? Take me away or something?"

"Maybe later, not now."

"What are you after, Jones? I don't understand."

"The only thing I'm any good at is looking for answers to questions I probably have no business asking."

"But why are you mixed up in all of this? What's your interest?"

"It's easier to shave if you can bear to look at yourself." My best John Wayne manner.

"You see, I was right about you. A knight-errant."

"I knew a man once, a tough little man, who had given his whole life to his ranch in mountainous country that was damn close to being wilderness. His grandfather and his father had ranched the same land. He and his wife had been together for forty years working a meager living off their land, and then she got cancer. The doctors said there wasn't anything they could do, but the rancher and his wife refused to give up, it just wasn't in them to quit, and he took her off to Mexico to one of those quacky laetrile clinics. When they got back home to the ranch they found that a forest fire was advancing toward their only patch of grazing meadow and that the federal people who were fighting the fire were planning to plow a fire line across their meadow. The topsoil up there was only an inch deep. One inch is an awfully shallow purchase to have on survival.

"I showed up to write a story about the fire when they were waiting to find out what was going to destroy them first, the cancer, the fire, or the feds. She offered me sandwiches and a beer, and out of politeness, you know, thinking that God, these people are about to lose everything, I can't take their food, I refused. The rancher—he was about sixty, a wiry, bowlegged little bundle of sinew and alert nerve endings—he spat in the dust. 'City feller,' he said to me, 'don't you know better than never to turn down food and drink when it's offered to you?'

"In the midst of all his own trouble he had the time to teach me real manners, which I suppose he was showing me is a different order of thing than politeness. The next morning before dawn—you could hardly tell dawn from dark, the smoke and dust from the fire was that thick—he went up to his meadow with his son and his foreman, this was after he had given his wife her morning injection and made her comfortable, and stood off the federal bulldozers. They just stood there at the edge of their one inch of good topsoil and defied the dozer drivers to keep coming. He saved his land. The thing was, and he never mentioned this to me, I found out later from his neighbors, he was going to have to sell the ranch anyway because the tax man was breathing down his neck and his wife's treatment was using up all their savings. The place was up for sale at the moment he was putting his body in front of those bulldozers to protect his meadow, and the only possible buyers were lumber companies who wanted the woodland and couldn't have cared less about the meadow. He had already lost everything but he protected it anyway. I guess you could say it was a Pyrrhic victory, but it was a victory. He was not about to let the bastards grind him down.

"That's the best answer I can give you. But listen, is your soon-to-be-ex-fiancé in the coke business as a regular thing?"

"No, I don't think so. A man with his own airplanes can do a lot of things. He's done them all."

"A Jerry-baby of all trades," I said. "Including murder?"

"*You* think so, too?"

"My daddy always taught me not to disagree with a beautiful woman who just made love to you in the afternoon." My daddy would have been mortified by the subject.

"I'm wonderful, I know." She traced my rib cage with a lazy finger. "What are we going to do next?"

"I have an idea."

She swung herself up on my lap facing me and began to kiss me, first on the eyelids, then on the cheeks, the ears. "Me, too," she said.

I must have dozed off afterward because it was almost dark the next time I spoke. "So if somebody could get in here they could get into the main part of the house through the interconnecting door?"

"Uh-huh." She was still half asleep, mumbling drowsily.

"Did Pressix ask you about that?"

"No, I don't think so."

"What did he ask you about?"

"About Harry's enemies," she said, fully awake now. "Where I had been. Whether I had heard or seen anything. Stuff like that."

"What was the relationship between your father and Thiesmann?"

"Dick? They went back a long way, they met in the war; you knew that, didn't you? In Europe? I kind of felt they were especially close, I'm talking about way back, before I was born. After the war Dick came back here to start training to take over the family newspaper and Harry went to New York on the fame-and-fortune trail. He never said too much about what happened there but I think he bombed. Flyboy Bombs in Big Apple, only it wasn't the Big Apple then. Then Dick hired him at *The Courier* and the column was boffo right off the bat. They fell out when Harry put something in the column about Dick's wife, I don't think it was anything really bad, just kind of naughty. The way I heard it Dick caught up with him at the lower bar at The Mark. He punched Harry out in front of a lot of people. Harry tried to laugh it off, you know, but after that he left *The Courier* and went over to *The Bulletin*. Do you think Dick's got something to do with all of this? I mean, that's the second time you've brought his name up."

"Maybe." I started to say more and then kept it to myself.

"You wouldn't let him get away with it if he had, would you?"

"No."

For an instant a more complete self showed itself in her lovely face, somebody hard and resolved shrugging aside the stylish, warm, sometimes flutter-brained girl. Then she shook her head as if to clear it of a primeval thought and kissed me full on the lips.

"Judy, did you know that your father was a homosexual?"

"Oh, *that*, I never believed that. He seemed kind of polymorphous to me, elfin, with those pointy little ears, you know, and so impeccable in everything. I wouldn't be surprised if there had been boys he wanted, but I don't think he would have done it. Are you sure?"

I nodded. "At least once, with one boy anyway."

"Do you think that had anything to do with why he was murdered?"

"It could have."

"Who was it?"

"I'm trying to find out."

"I want you to let me know if you do, Jones. It's important to me."

"Okay. Hey, what time is it?"

"About nine, nine-thirty." She shrugged and snuggled closer to me. "You don't have to go, do you? Stay here tonight, I don't want to be alone."

"I've got to meet a man. About a thing."

"Oh, hell, Jones." She pouted. But she walked me to the door in an unbelted kimono and kissed me goodbye in a way that meant hello.

16

They were right on time. Beans opened the passenger door and moved to the back seat, and I got in beside Wagner.

"Take 101 to 280," I told him. The tower of the Ferry Building was lit up for the night, shining brightly against the dark lapping silence of the Bay. It was clear and the lights strung along the roadway of the bridge sparkled like a jeweled bracelet. We left the bridge behind, driving south. My stomach was hollow and busy.

There was a full clip in the Walther and another in the pocket of my windbreaker. I wasn't accustomed to the pull of the shoulder strap or to the weight of the gun where it hung beneath the crook of my arm and I kept shifting, trying to get comfortable. It was more than the unaccustomed presence of the hardware that made me jumpy. I kept looking at the people in other cars, wondering where *they* were off to.

Wagner was silent until we had rounded Hospital Curve and picked up Highway 280. "You have what you want from Mr. Wallach," he said, never taking his eyes off the road. "You got a meet when this is over with."

"A ways to go," I said, not sure myself if I meant the distance we had to travel before we reached Stoneface and the rock-'n'-roller, or what might happen after we got there.

Short of the airstrip where the road passed through a

grove of eucalyptus trees, I told Wagner to slow down and cut his headlights. We rolled to the top of the airport service road and got out of the car. The sounds of the night—the leaves rustling in the trees, the crickets, even the hum coming off the overhead power lines—seemed unnaturally loud in the absence of the whooshing roar of moving automobiles. All my senses were heightened. The tangy eucalyptus scent was powerful.

At the end of the service road was the terminal building, visible only as a darker shape against the horizon, except for a light in one window. I nodded in its direction and whispered, "There."

Wagner and Beans took their guns out. I left mine where it was. We approached through the damp grass, the earth muffling and hiding our footfalls. About ten yards in front of the terminal my foot caught something and I stumbled and almost fell. I bent down to see what had tripped me and found a soft patch of bare, loose earth that looked as if it had recently been dug up. I could hear a radio playing in the terminal. Somewhere far away a dog barked.

With a motion of his gun Wagner directed Beans around the back of the building. We crouched low and headed toward the lit window, keeping ourselves beneath the line of vision of anybody inside. When we were up against the shingles I cautiously raised my head to the level of the sill. Stoneface was sitting at the table reading a girlie magazine, wearing the same black Ultrasuede jacket and a tie held by a jade clasp. At his elbow was a mirror across which were laid out long, looping lines of cocaine, a full gram vial, a single-edge razor, a brass straw, an open pack of Pall Malls, a Zippo lighter, and a can of Bud Light with the ring pulled up but not off. I felt a surge of glad bitterness at the sight of the rock-'n'-roller stretched out on an old cracked leather couch with his hands behind his head and his snakeskin boots crossed at the ankles. He was staring at the ceiling, singing along with Merle Haggard on the radio.

In his grotesque, electrically amplified voice Stoneface

said, "Turn off that hayseed puke and turn on some music, godamnit."

The rock-'n'-roller didn't budge.

Wagner caught my attention and motioned me toward the front door. He had seen Beans in a back window signaling he was ready, but I had been so riveted by my hatred for the two men inside I hadn't noticed. Silently, my muscles straining with the effort of remaining noiseless, I made it to the door. I made the thumbs-up sign. Wagner fired his gun, hitting the mirror on which the coke was spread out. He shouted something unintelligible to me. Beans must have fired too because I heard a second explosion. I was throwing myself against the door and twisting the knob. I crashed into the room just as the rock-'n'-roller was getting to his feet with his gun in his hand. I pounded his chin with my shoulder, the full force of my two hundred pounds behind the blow. His head snapped back, the gun flew out of his grasp, and he collapsed across the couch. I yanked him up by the shirt front and was about to hit him full in the face with my balled fist when I realized he was offering no resistance. I released his shirt and he fell back onto the couch groaning. The sonofabitch. I yanked off his fine boots and carried them over to the table where Stoneface was standing with both hands clasped on the top of his head. There was shattered glass and white powder in his hair and his eyebrows. I searched until I found the razor blade and slashed at the boots until ribbons of snakeskin hung loose. I threw the boots at the rock-'n'-roller, hitting the wall above him. One boot landed on his chest.

Beans had his gun—an enormous gun—leveled at Stoneface, while Wagner began to open drawers and closets.

"You're looking for a brown leather satchel the size of a traveling case," I said.

The rock-'n'-roller was groaning and twitching on the couch.

Beans spoke for the first time. "Broke his collarbone." He was smiling that conspiratorial smile of his.

"Did I?" I went over to Stoneface and put my hands on his shoulders and forced him back down onto his chair.

"He got a gun?" Beans asked.

I made him stand up again and patted him until I found a pistol stuck into his belt at the small of his back.

"His ankles," said Beans.

Sure enough I found a second, smaller weapon taped beneath his pants leg.

"You talk good," I told Beans.

He grinned at me.

"Got it," Wagner said, pulling Yollo's case out from under the couch where the rock-'n'-roller was still groaning. Wagner unzipped it, looked inside, and rezipped it. "Do it," he told Beans.

Beans waved his large gun toward Stoneface, indicating he should get down on the floor. I could see sweat break out all around his eyes and I watched a dark stain grow on the front of his pants.

"No," I said. "You got what you wanted. Let me handle them."

"You want to do it?" Wagner asked.

"Yeah." There was a telephone on the wall. I went to it and dialed.

"Police," said a female voice. There were beeping sounds on the line indicating that the call was being taped.

"I have an emergency message for Pressix in Homicide. Tell him the suspects he's seeking in the murder of Yollo Current are waiting for him to come pick them up." I gave her precise directions. When she began to ask me questions I hung up. For good measure I ripped the phone out of the wall, something I had always wanted to do. It came loose rather easily, dangling by a single wire. I would have liked to see the whole sequence again, beginning with my tackle of the rock-'n'-roller, on slow motion replay. Maybe the best part of being a professional athlete in America wasn't the money, or the adulation, but the limitless opportunity to watch your own best moments.

Beans found a coil of heavy rope and we trussed the two of them up.

"Wipe your prints off the case," I said to Wagner, "and leave it." We transferred the clear plastic packets bulging with white powder to a brown paper bag. I had never seen or held that quantity of cocaine, but I felt no wish to keep any of it for myself.

When Wagner was reaching for the last packet I said, "No, leave one in the satchel."

"I doubt my associates will be pleased about all the different things we're leaving behind here."

"Leave one, man. The cops'll need it to make their case. Leave their guns, too. The ballistics will match up on Yollo. And maybe Shugart, too. Will the ballistics match up on Shugart?" I asked Stoneface. He didn't say anything. "Will they?" I said, moving closer to him. Still he didn't speak.

"Let me," Beans said. I could see the fright again in Stoneface's face.

"Sure, you ask him."

Through his voicebox Stoneface said, "Ask Cole about that."

"Enough bullshit," Wagner said. "Let's get out of here." He turned to Stoneface. "You do right with the cops or when you get inside you'll wish you died here."

Before I left I slapped the rock-'n'-roller gently on his cheek until he opened his eyes. "Didn't your mama teach you any better manners than to point guns at taxi drivers?"

We jogged up the roadway this time, not caring how much noise we made, and Wagner drove fast until we reached the main highway where we fell in with the traffic flow and its blessed ceaseless anonymity.

When they dropped me at my place I stood on the sidewalk, too restless and exhilarated to go upstairs. I began to walk east across Broadway. The bars and clubs were closed for the night, and the only people on the street were some bedraggled hookers and insomniacs. At that hour of the early morning every face you passed looked like it was on the lam from itself. Near Mubuhay Gardens there were still a few punks congregating in their studded leathers and chains. I approached them with a new sense not of bravery but of defiance. Probably my defiance, some hint of which must have shown in my tilt or my gait, was a provocation that served to increase the chance of their challenging me. The hunter and the hunted always knew each other. Didn't they, Buddy?

I walked a long way, finally sitting down beside the Lefty O'Doul drawbridge above China Basin Channel. Just up the road at the Tic Tock diner there were cop cars and taxis parked outside. I was suddenly famished. I hadn't eaten all day, but I didn't want to meet anybody I knew so I walked back to Red's Java House and ate hotcakes and sausages with the longshoremen stoking up to go to work and lingered over coffee, not leaving until it was light and the first commuters were pouring into the city, swelling it like a leech.

Nellie was in the press room on the third floor of the Hall of Justice, a cardboard cup of coffee trembling in his hands.

"Pressix made a big pinch in Burlingame a couple of hours ago," I said.

"Impossible. Out of his jurisdiction."

"Jurisdiction? What's that got to do with anything? It was two guys who killed a dealer named Yollo Current."

"The one they found out at Ocean Beach?"

"They may not be ready to say anything about it, but it ties in with the Shugart murder."

He was on his feet and halfway out the door before I finished. Over his skinny shoulder he said, "Even-Steven."

Not by a long shot, not yet I wasn't.

ARRESTS IN SHUGART MURDER. The headline on *The Courier* was a page-wide banner. SUSPECTS SEIZED ON PENINSULA. Nellie's story recounted the arrests of Randy Pendleton—the rock-'n'-roller—and William Frimmer—Stoneface—by a combined force of city cops and Burlingame police. It said that information on the whereabouts of the suspects had come to Pressix from "a tipster."

~~~~ 17 ~~~~

ARRESTS IN SHUGART MURDER. The headline on *The Courier* was a page-wide banner. SUSPECTS SEIZED ON PENINSULA. Nellie's story recounted the arrests of Randy Pendleton—the rock-'n'-roller—and William Frimmer—Stoneface—by a combined force of city cops and Burlingame police. It said that information on the whereabouts of the suspects had come to Pressix from "a tipster."

Pendleton, it continued, had his collarbone broken in a criminal falling-out with Frimmer and was in General Hospital under heavy guard. Pressix was quoted as saying that Shugart had been killed when he interrupted the suspects while they were burglarizing his house. Their past criminal records were itemized. No mention was made of cocaine, nor of the suspects being neatly wrapped up like early Christmas presents when the police arrived to arrest them. Inside the paper was an editorial praising the police in general and Pressix in particular for a swift and successful investigation and for their "assiduously cultivated sources in the criminal underworld."

"While the case against these two career criminals is not to be prejudged," the editorial said, "it is with understandable pride and a deep sense of justice being done that we applaud the arrest of two of society's moral midgets who allegedly, and for no greater reason than base greed, murdered one of the city's giants.''

I thought of calling Judy but it didn't seem necessary. She would have known by now that Frimmer and Pendleton had murdered her father.

By the time I reached the Hall it was past five o'clock and nearly empty. There wasn't even a recruit manning the metal detector. I passed through it anyway and sure enough tripped the pulse. Nobody stopped me. I was alone in the elevator. The graffito said, ''Nigers die.'' It was signed with a swastika. The wide marble-floored corridor echoed my footfalls. Pressix was on the telephone, his redwood-size legs propped across the edge of his desk, holding an unlit cigar.

''Yes, ma'am,'' he said respectfully. ''Thank you, ma'am. I appreciate it and my family will too. I certainly will, ma'am. Thank you.'' He hung up and without looking at me said, '' 'Bout time.''

''The mayor,'' I said. ''What's it going to be, gold or silver?''

''Silver. No direct danger to my person. But she want to do it herself. With my wife and family bein' there.''

I turned and started to walk back the way I had come.

''Where you think you goin', Sonny?''

I kept walking.

''Henry!''

My fists were opening and clenching in a slow rhythm. His feet slammed to the floor. He leaned toward me across his desk. ''You so fuckin' dumb it's a miracle you can fuckin' tie youh laces without no training manual.''

''You *know*,'' I said. ''You know better. Pendleton and Frimmer are plankton, bottom of the food chain. You know about the coke deal and Jerry Cole and Thiesmann. Hell, you even had a nice little chat with Thiesmann the night of the murder.''

''I tell you what I know. Man called me and tol' me he was there. When I get over there he got one of the top lawyers in this town with him. He was cooperative, they were friends, him and the victim, he went up there on just a friendly visit. All he ask for is to keep his name out of it, which he could probably do without no help from me. No reason not to do what the man asks. How many chances you get to do favors for an important man like that?

"Yeah," Pressix continued, "and I know about how you snatch his son and act like some sort of tough guy. I forget about that, too. We all gotta forget what's best forgot. Why dontcha face the factual way of things, Sonny? Climb down off your high fuckin' horse and look at this world down where the rest of us standing?"

"Facts? It's the facts I'm talking about. The facts say bullshit."

"You gonna set us all straight again, Sonny? Last time you landed ass-under on the sidewalk."

"Man, you must have cared once. Or is that just more high horse talk the way you see it?"

"You thinkin' that way, it put you on the street pushing hack. For peanuts. Now I'm drawin' thirty-three-eight-fifty each annum, that don't count in the overtime. I got more safe deposits you got matchin' socks. I drive a Porsche. Nine two four. Old lady drive a Merc station wagon. This year's model. My boy, he drive a Mustang down there at UCLA. G'wan, Sonny, tell me how to live right."

What did I want him to do, after all? "Is the case closed?"

He held up his long fingers and ticked them off one at a time. "Suspects. Weapon. Ballistics match up with the gun we found on Frimmer. Motive, a little shaky. Far as we concerned, what else we need?"

"I think the jade statue from Shugart's place may be buried out in front of the air terminal," I said. "There's a patch there that's been dug up recently."

"We check it out."

"You going to charge them for Yollo, too?"

"Well, we got some good solid evidence there. Not as much as maybe there started with, but solid. I think we take this one step at a time, least that's the way the D.A. is doing his thinkin'. It ain't my decision to make but I don't see nothin' wrong with that." He got up and went over to a file case where a hot plate was warming a pot of coffee. "Want some?" He held up the pot.

"Yeah."

He brought two cups to his desk and put mine down in front of me. It was sludge, tepid sludge.

"We lookin' for Cole. But I got to hand it to you, Sonny. Those are pretty tough boys you put youh move on."

I didn't say anything. I wanted to reach for a cigarette but resisted the impulse.

"Got a smoke?" Pressix said. "This old thing gotten kind of mean tastin'." The tip of his cigar was chewed into a gloopy flat thing. He put it down on his desk.

I took out a cigarette and tossed it to him and lit one myself.

"How you do it?" he asked, exhaling.

"I had help."

"Huh." There was a silence. "What kind of cigarette this?"

"Exports."

"Huh. Good smoke. Knowin' how you are a law abiding citizen, tellin' the rest of us ouh duties, you wouldn't be messin' 'round with no narcotics pushers, now would you? I want you to stay both feet inside the law, you hear me, Sonny."

"I'm not through with this, even if you are."

"You listen, listen, listen, takin' notes in your mind, but you don't hear none too good. I got a boss. My boss, he got a boss. My boss's boss, he report directly to the Chief. Now the Chief, he got a private line on his desk so the Mayor she can just pick up and talk to him when she feelin' blue and lonesome. The Mayor, she eat dinner with all sorts of people and their lawyers. You gotta try to understand these things, Sonny."

"What is that I'm not hearing, that your hands are tied?"

"You asked me, is the case closed?"

"Yeah, and you said it was."

He shook his huge head. "You just as dumb as you ever been. What I said was, what else we need?"

18

Pressix had surprised me, but no more than my own vehemence about continuing to ask questions and look for answers. After all, with Frimmer and Pendleton out of the game Yollo was revenged, and so was I. Shugart's murder was solved, it was yesterday's news, a story that had run its course and become a strip of microfilm in the newspaper library, what had been called the morgue until the pinheads gave the nomenclature a corporate cleansing. The morgue is what it was, though, final resting place of dead news. Now I was like someone who had followed a route toward an unknown destination only to come to the edge of the map. I had only instinct left to guide me, that tug which said there's more to be found, and you still don't know what it is, do you, Mr. Jones?

Before long I was following my feet across Columbus Avenue to Tosca's and a cold beer. What possible difference did it make to me, really, if Thiesmann, and Shugart while he was still alive, and the mayor, and the police brass were all content with partial answers, convenient solutions that put a couple of creeps in the slammer and kept the game going? Wasn't that how poker was played, clean out the losers and keep dealing the cards until there were only winners at the table? And, God, they were good at the game in everybody's favorite city. With the way it glorified its past history of shanghaied sailors and vigilante lynch mobs, its robber barons building their palatial homes on top of Nob Hill and its notorious madams with alleys named after them—*The Courier* itself backed on Minna Alley—you would have thought that the mob would have San Francisco as wrapped up as New York, Hollywood, Las Vegas. But the bosses had never managed to cross the Golden Gate, even the Bonnanos in their exile did business out of drab, dreadful San Jose, an hour south. It seemed unlikely unless you knew how the Frisco cops had kept the streets as safe as tax shelters.

Joseph came over and wordlessly wiped my ashtray clean. He picked up my nearly empty bottle and poured the last golden drops into my glass. Then he turned and bent over to take a new bottle glowing with condensed coolness out of an oak refrigerator cabinet and popped the cap with a deft snap of his wrist. With his other hand he put a fresh napkin in front of me while he was placing the green beer bottle precisely in the middle of a coaster. It was all done with an economy of motion, a purity of action, that could only come from pride and long practice.

"House buys," he said. He didn't stick around to discuss it with me, nor to be thanked, nor to strike up an idle conversation. He had read my face and knew I wanted to be left alone.

Joseph would understand why I kept pushing. You did what you did as well as you could. Each time you did less than that you were diminished, and the diminutions were like dead cells, they were never revitalized or replaced. Sometimes it seemed that self-respect could only be had by the foolish insistence on reaching for what would be forever beyond your power to catch hold of. But between playing the fool, and indifference's little deaths, what choice was there?

I sensed the presence of somebody standing behind my stool. I took a long swallow of my beer.

"Mr. Wallach wants you to join him for supper." I turned to face Paul Wagner wearing another baggy, neutral off-the-rack suit—or maybe it was the same one—his pale eyes swimming like oysters on the half shell behind his thick lenses. Over his shoulder Beans was nodding at me. Pavarotti was yodeling on the jukebox.

"Beans, m'boy," I said, strangely glad to see him. "Say anything good lately?"

He gave me that inclusive, secretive grin of his.

"You couldn't be more right," I told him. To Wagner I said, "When?"

"Now."

I had no objection. Off the bar stool and onto the map again.

Albert's, on Broadway above the tunnel, was not that sort of California restaurant where the waiter tells you his name is Kurt and then describes the specials of the day down to the last sprig of tarragon while you try to decide what to do with your face. Albert's did not have a talking menu; it retained its old-fashioned faith in print. The restaurant was a medium-sized, squarish room permeated with the faint smell of beef being flamed. It was furnished with deep red banquettes, chandeliers, and square columns faced with mirrors. Wagner walked me as far as a corner banquette and then departed without a word.

I was left facing somebody with a smallish head above wide, round shoulders. His hair was slicked back in a long, flat arc and his oval face was bland and smooth except for small, deepset, hooded eyes and clumps of muscle bunched at the top of his jawbone. He was dressed in quiet, expensive clothes suitable for a chief executive officer, just the right sort of man for the job of softening up San Francisco's drug market for a takeover bid. Somebody who could go over the heads of the police directly to the money laundries at the top of the financial district towers.

The table was exceptionally wide, but his hand met mine more than halfway across. He was as tall as I was.

"You play basketball?" I asked him when we were both settled at the table.

"Indiana."

"A good basketball state."

He nodded. "You?"

"I was never much of a joiner. Pickup games."

We ordered drinks and steaks. Wallach liked his rare. He didn't look at the menu before he ordered. There seemed to be something almost subaquatic about his appearance; he resembled a dolphin or a torpedo.

"You're new around here."

"Some associates from the Midwest thought I could help them get based out here."

"Ah. How's it going?"

"No negative feedback from them at this point in time. Some glitches, as you know." The hooded eyes closed momentarily, the muscles in his jaws clenched and unclenched, and his thin lips were pulled out and down at the corners. A smile, I think.

"Yollo was a glitch?"

"I'm sorry about that. We employed him because he was known as a reliable middleman. Let me assure you that we had nothing whatsoever to do with his demise. I think you have enough input to deduce the bottom line there. He gambled, he lost."

"I've been wondering how come you sent Wagner and Beans around to see me in the first place. I mean, what made you think I'd know how to find the stuff you were looking for?"

"You did know, so the input I had was good input. I'm sure you'd agree that there's nothing more useful in doing business than good input."

I shook my head. "Not really."

"No?"

"What about good people?"

His expression remained noncommittal, evaluating me as I assessed him. "An essential configuration, but the most error-prone. My people tell me, for instance, that the shipment we recovered was under inventory, at your insistence. And not to suggest any criticism, but certain perishable goods are better disposed of than put in storage."

"I'm not in the habit of killing inconvenient people, as much as it might be appealing where those two were concerned."

"Don't misunderstand, your contribution was valuable to us. That's why I've kept up our end of the agreement. We're prepared to be supportive of your goals, if we can be."

"To tell you the truth, I'm not certain just what it is I want to know. There's a lot more to this than Frimmer and Pendleton holding up Shugart and then killing him almost as an afterthought, the police version. How did they know about Yollo's delivery? That's someplace to start."

"It has to be understood between us that we're communicating privately," Wallach said. "You're programmed to be a very aggressive and troublesome journalist. I'm certain you understand we seek no publicity. The things you and I dialogue, they won't go any further?"

"As far as I'm concerned this is entirely a private matter."

"I accept that." He looked at me from beneath his hooded eyelids set deep into his skull. It was a look I would have been terminally foolish to forget. "The parameters were that Cole was planning to snatch the delivery," he said, speaking softly so that I had to lean forward to be sure of catching every word. "That was the reason for the presence of his two subordinates. The daughter was Yollo's intended recipient. It all went down the way it did because she and he were late for the meet. Cole's subordinates showed up before they did. When they didn't find the goods where Cole had said they would be—and I should explain that he was intending to take her out of the house after the transaction so she wouldn't be in the way of his freelance operation—they panicked. The rest is speculation based on the best data available to me. It could be that her father came to investigate, or that they stumbled across him. When he couldn't tell them what they wanted to know they deresolved him. Most probably they saw no other options; he could identify them. He may have met them previously through Cole."

I didn't want to believe what he was telling me about

Judy any more than I wanted to be stabbed in the heart. "You're sure she was the recipient?"

"Absolutely. The order was placed with us, remember. Here are our steaks."

"Why would she be dealing?"

He looked at me as if I were very stupid. "Everybody does business for the same reason. And the girl is a thrill seeker, too." What he said made sense, both about Judy's nature and her wanting more ready cash than Harry Shugart probably made available to her.

We remained silent while the waiter put down our dinners and departed. I had lost my appetite but I didn't want Wallach to know that, so I cut my steak and began to chew. Wallach tucked into his filet without any hesitation. There was clear polish on his manicured nails. He held his utensils in the European fashion, keeping the fork in his left hand and using the knife to manipulate the food.

"Where did you learn to eat that way?"

"London," he said, wiping his mouth. "I took an advanced degree at the School of Economics. On a grant, a privately endowed grant. You like your steak?"

"Very much," I told him, forcing myself to take another bite. "Don't you think that Frimmer and Pendleton are going to give up Jerry Cole to the cops? It's the only deal they can hope to cut."

"They already have," he said, heaping sour cream onto his baked potato.

"And they could give up Judy, too."

"Yes, but that won't get them any return."

"Why not? With her father dead, what's her juice?"

"I don't believe her father was her protector. But we're finally accessing your priorities." Again his eyelids drooped, the jaw muscles clenched, and the mouth briefly widened. He might just have been chewing, but I thought it was another smile: he understood why this question was important to me.

"You know who is?" I asked him.

"I have my ideas. No more than that."

"Well?"

"From the available data I would say your base for learning conclusively is better than ours. I don't want to lead you into an error mode. You know, of course, that there's a contract out on Cole?"

"You're going to tell me that Judy Shugart put it out?"

He shrugged as if to say, who else?

"Have you ever considered that a man of your capabilities," Wallach said, pushing away his empty plate, "is underutilizing himself driving a taxicab?"

I couldn't help smiling. "Once or twice."

"We've postmortemed the deviations from our spreadsheet for retrieving our goods. It seems you displayed leadership qualities and we already were aware that you had considerable skill and knowledge of the territory." He shot his starched white cuffs and turned his Rolex until it was placed to his liking. "Organizationally speaking, you could put your considerable assets to better use."

"Yeah, but I've never played organized ball," I told him. "I'm not a team player."

"I thought that was what you'd say." He signaled for the waiter. "Dessert with your coffee?"

"Be-en?"

"Oh, Peter. I'm supposed to call you, not the other way around."

"Yes, but Ben, there are people who are trying to speak with you. For two days you have not asked for your messages."

"I've been busy. Who called?"

"Miss Shugart called. Twice, Ben. She is a very poetical girl. Yesterday's message was, 'Coffee isn't so sweet without my sugar.' That is very nice, don't you think so?"

"Very." It made me more wary than warm, though. "What else, Peter?"

"A Miss A-reetha, Ben."

"Aretha, huh?"

"Yes. She said to call her, it might be important."

"Okay, Peter. Keep 'em coming."

"That is all, Ben. There are no more."

Rather than return my calls I rang Pressix. Somebody else answered and yelled for him to pick it up.

"Pressix," he rumbled.

"You got a fugitive warrant out on Jerry Cole?"

"Henry?"

"No, Humpty Dumpty."

"Did. Don't no more."

"Why not?"

141

"Showed up dead a few hours ago in San Berdoo. What brought me into the office. Shot dead in the back of the head in a motel near the airport down there. Local cops saw our APB, gave us a call."

"Damn."

"Didn't know you were friends."

"Mutual interests is more like it. Who did it?"

"San Berdoo's problem, Sonny, not ouhs."

"Yeah, right. Jurisdictions. How could I forget?"

"By the by," he said. "That statue? Good clear prints."

I stayed by the phone when we finished talking. I guess it came of having been a reporter, I didn't merely make phone calls, I worked the phone. Looking for a story, or checking one out, I could spend entire days on the telephone, filling scratch sheets with numbers, notes, doodles. It was a form of thinking. I usually didn't know what I really thought until I heard myself say it out loud, or wrote it down. I picked up a pencil—a Dixon Ticonderoga Number One, extra-soft—and began idly to mark up a pad of newsprint seconds. I wrote "Sugar" and around it made a cube. Then I made a series of three interlocking circles, like the Ballantine logo. Beneath that I wrote 1234567890987654321. Back to the beginning. I made a second set of interlocking circles. This time I labeled them. Inside the first I wrote "Shugart." Inside the third, "Thiesmann." The middle one, linked to both the others, was Ricky. Off to one side I drew a gun with a little cloud above it that said, "Bang. Bang." I went back to the first set of circles and couldn't think of any labels for them. I put my legs across the edge of the table, crossing them at the ankles, and scratched my crown, tousling my hair. Once again I labeled the first circle Shugart. And the third Thiesmann. The interconnecting circle remained blank. Then I enclosed it in a square. The square became a cube. She answered on the first ring.

"Yes?"

"I'm sorry about Jerry."

"Oh, Jones, it's you. It's all right. I'll be okay." She sniffled. "It wouldn't be so bad if I hadn't dropped him.

It wouldn't be so bad then.'' The sniffles turned to quiet sobs.

"You want me to come over?''

"No. No. It's something I've got to handle. You understand, don't you? Soon, but not now.''

"Yes, okay. Anything I can do, let me know.''

"That's sweet. G'night, Jonesy.''

I rushed downstairs two at a time and got into the car without bothering to remove the ticket from under the wiper. It flapped and waved all the way out to Pacific Heights. Much as I still wanted to entrust myself to Judy Shugart I knew she wasn't the sort of woman to be alone with whatever she was feeling, whether it was grief or shock at having successfully paid to have Jer-baby killed.

I left the car parked around the corner and approached the house from the other side of the street. In the deep darkness of an overhanging tree I stood for a moment to see if anybody was stirring at 3670 Jackson and then crossed toward it cautiously. The lights were all off upstairs and there was a Jaguar sedan in the driveway. The lilacs lining the flagstone path at the side of the house were night-fragrant. I could see a light on in her apartment, so I got down on my hands and knees and crawled toward the window. The shutters were closed but some of the slats had small gaps between them. I craned my neck trying to get a glimpse of what was going on inside. The first thing I saw besides carpeting was a man's oxblood shoes. Very expensive shoes, wingtips. Likewise the dark pinstripe suit legs. I could only see as far up as his knees. He was sitting on the white couch. I put my ear close to the glass but I didn't hear voices. I backed away and slid off my boots and in my stockinged feet shimmied up the stone wall that separated the path from the adjoining property. Cautiously I raised my head level with the top of the window. The shutters were not a perfect fit, and I could see down into the room. She was on the couch with her legs drawn up under her. Beside her was the man with the well-made shoes. His shirt was an Oxford button-down and his tie had club stripes. The way in which their bodies were resting against each other bespoke a familiarity, a belonging together. They had been silent but now he looked down at her and said something.

She didn't respond. Her eyes were closed. Very gently he removed her weight and eased her down full length onto the couch. He crossed out of my line of vision and then returned with a pillow and a knit comforter. He lifted her head, her golden hair shimmying loose, and slipped the pillow in beneath, and then he covered her. She burrowed into the couch and opened an eye and said one word, I could not hear what.

I leaped off the wall and retrieved my boots. Carrying them in one hand I went down to the back end of the path, past her door, where the shadows were deepest. I wedged myself as far into the darkness as I could and tried to make my breath silent. My heart was thumping, my thoughts were a shocked and bitter jumble, and my molars were clenched so tight I thought they would squeak.

The door opened. From inside he said, "You're certain you'll be safe here by yourself?"

Drowsily she answered, "It's over. I'm fine."

"I'll call in the morning," he said, starting out.

"G'night, Daddy."

"Goodnight, Princess." He pulled the door shut behind him, twisting the handle to ensure that it was locked. Then he walked away up the path. I heard the door of the Jaguar open and close. The motor purred immediately into life and he drove away. I felt a sudden vertigo and for a moment I thought I was going to swoon.

It was a long time since I had seen him, but the things he thought about me were never long out of my mind. Suddenly it came back to me in a flush of shame and anger that I had told Judy I was going to make him regret what he had done to me. I hadn't known he was doing it to me still. Richard Cornelius Thiesmann. Daddy?

20

My legs felt like intimations of varicose veins as I walked up and down Telegraph Hill one slow step at a time. North Beach had a lazy Sunday feel, people strolling at their leisure digesting big late breakfasts. On the sidewalk in front of Iteli's bookstore a cluster of people were holding plastic wine cups and talking. I didn't want to face the loneliness of my apartment so I wandered over to see what was going on. There was a handprinted sign in the bookstore window. "Meet Jessica Gage. The author of *Ordinary Losses* will be signing books from 1 p.m. to 4 p.m. today." I remembered then that Joel Petry had suggested I stop by. I put my face up against the plate glass but all I could see was a reflection of myself and the street behind me. I held up a hand to block out the sunlight, creating a small shaded transparency.

The author was at a table behind stacks of her books, people gathered around her trying to get her attention, all of them drinking from the little plastic cups and talking. She turned from one person to another as they demanded attention. She was being asked to sign a book and, as she did, two bracelets slid down her slim wrist and collided at her palm. Her eyes were focused on some middle distance, suggesting shyness or discomfort, but she had an engaging, spontaneous smile that she turned on each person who approached. I had the feeling that I had seen her

145

before but I couldn't say where. Just then she looked directly toward me. My reflex was to drop my eyes, but she held her gaze steadily. I could have sworn I knew her, and yet I was equally sure I had never met her. Well, it didn't matter.

I walked back toward my place and then on past it and bought an ice cream cone from the kid in the sidewalk stand. He remembered what flavor I liked and it earned him a quarter tip, the way it always did. The cool sweetness of the ice cream was a kind of balm. I had known better than to let myself care about Judy Shugart, but I was lonely and vain enough to think I could outrace the shadow that was my own knowledge. Now I was paying for my mistake by facing decisions I would have to make but would rather not.

I started toward Tosca's and remembered it wasn't open on Sunday. I didn't really want to drink. Then I took a step toward my Chinese red door again and stopped, not wanting to be alone with my thoughts. My legs were probably too old to carry me up the stairs anyway. Quiet and solitude were no salvation today. What the hell, I moseyed on into the bookstore still licking my ice cream.

What had been a murmur became a small roar once I was inside. I edged past the room where Jessica Gage was signing books and where the crush was the greatest and down the steps to the basement. The usual bookstore smell of paper and cogitation today had a lot of perfume and tobacco added to it. I tried browsing but it was no good, I wasn't interested in any of the books I picked up. I considered the word aimless, its on-target accuracy. I trudged back upstairs. The noise level had dropped to an excited curious whisper and several people were standing on tiptoes craning to get a look at what was happening near Jessica Gage where a single voice was raised abrasively. There were advantages to being as tall as I am, one of them being that I can see over crowds. Another—the thought passed like a fleeting stab of self-pity—was that if I had kids I could hoist them on my shoulders to watch parades. *Ordinary Losses*. Its author, I could see, was being harangued by two guys in studded leathers.

". . . a tank of bullshit," yelled one of them, who was thin and had lank, unwashed streaky blond hair. I moved closer through the crowd. Jessica Gage responded but I couldn't make out what she said.

The other punk, he was a porker with a pink, broad forehead, barechested under his studded leather vest, snatched one of the books off the pile on the table. She reached for it with a protective gesture. He began to thumb through it, sneering and bending pages.

A man in the crowd said, "Cut that out." Both punks turned threateningly in his direction. He shut his mouth. A woman in a red caftan said, "You are behaving like beasts. How dare you!" Her face was flushed nearly the same color as her caftan. The tall blond punk put his face close to hers and made as if to spit. She gasped and looked wildly around her for help. A few people offered scolding words but nobody stepped forward.

"Kindly replace that book and stop intimidating all these people." It was Jessica Gage. I hadn't realized she was British.

"Words are dead, manners are putrefaction." It was the squat, shirtless punk. He slammed the volume onto the table, upsetting a bottle of wine. "*You* are all fuckin' dead and you don't even fuckin' know it."

"You are being very rude." Jessica Gage was more outraged than frightened.

"Oooh, pardon me." It was a mockery.

"Pardon *me*," I said. I had reached the front of the anxious, curious circle of bookish people, all of them mesmerized by the possibility of violence crackling there.

The three of them all turned to me, the punks with arrogant swings of their bodies. There were livid blotches of deep pink in Jessica Gage's cheeks.

"What did you say, asshole?" It was the tall one.

"I wonder if you would hold this for me?" I extended the ice cream cone toward him.

"Whaaa?"

"I asked you to hold my ice cream cone."

"What the fuck are you talking about?" This was the squat one.

I opened my hand and let the ice cream drop. Both their gazes followed it down. Before it had hit with a shlurpy plop I took hold of the tall one's arm and twisted it behind his back just short of the breaking point. He howled in pain. Without letting go of him I kicked his partner in the kneecap with the full force of my weight. He fell to the floor, writhing. All my fury had broken loose. I left him on the floor and ran the other one through the crowd, people stumbling in their haste to make way, with his arm still twisted up behind him. When we reached the door I pulled him in closer to me and then kicked him as hard as I could, sending him sprawling into the street on all fours.

I hurried back inside. The other one had half-risen, grasping his knee with both hands. As I approached him he reached into his pants pocket and pulled out a knife, which he opened with a flick of his wrist. I kicked his forearm savagely and he screamed when he dropped the knife. I grabbed a fistful of greasy hair and hauled him toward the door, his bad leg dragging. He tried to swing at me but I used his own momentum to spin him around so I could plant my foot in the same place where I had punted the first one. He half-limped, half-ran up the block.

Everybody was talking at once. Joel Petry came over. "Whew! You okay?"

"Never better." I meant it, too.

"My God," he said.

"Hell, we can't have this kind of thing going on right here on our block."

"Maybe I should call the cops?"

"What for?"

"In case they come back with reinforcements or something."

"Up to you. Just don't mention my name to them if you do, okay?"

He smiled. "A stranger on a white horse?"

I smiled too. People were staring at me and whispering

excitedly. Jessica Gage was coming toward us. She was slim and wore her reddish-brown hair straight. It didn't quite reach her shoulders. There was around her a remarkable air of poise and familiarity.

"Are you hurt?" she asked.

"No. You okay?"

"Yes, of course. We haven't met, have we? I'm Jessica Gage." She extended a hand.

"Ben Henry," I said. Her palm was dry and firm. The way she held my hand was feminine but not self-conscious. "I'm sorry to have broken up your party."

"A good thing you did, I should think." She smiled engagingly. "Those barbarians were becoming extremely tiresome."

"Yeah. Well, tiresome barbarians are a specialty of mine."

"I dread to think what your other specialities might be." She pronounced it with all the syllables distinct: spesh-ee-ahl-ih-tees.

I laughed, not at what she said so much as at the way she said it.

"Mind you, our book parties at home are a good deal less eventful."

Joel Petry said, "Ours only get out of hand when Ben drops by, Jessica. The rest of the time they're as dull as sand."

"You're known here, then?" she asked me.

"A neighbor. I have a place upstairs."

"I have the most curious sensation of having met you elsewhere."

I was astonished to hear her say what I had been thinking when I first saw her through the window. "I was looking through the window a little while back, maybe you noticed me then."

"Yes, that was when I thought I knew you, when I first saw you at the window."

I don't know why but what we were saying seemed charged with significance. "Maybe another life." The flippancy was intended to disguise my embarrassment.

"Yes." She was contemplative. "Do you suppose there were other lives, then?"

"I've really never thought about it. I don't see why not."

"We've got a collection of books on mysticism and re-incarnation if you want to get into it any deeper," Petry said.

Jessica Gage blushed furiously. I shuffled my feet.

"You're new in America?" I asked her.

"I'm on a writer-in-residence program at Berkeley, you see. And Mr. Petry was kind enough to arrange for this little party and, well, the rest is just tiresome barbarians. Oh, pardon me, the excitement has deprived me of my manners. May I replace your ice cream?"

I laughed as if it were the funniest thing I had ever heard, and she blushed but laughed too. In fact, everything she said, even the most serious things, seemed to have some laughter hidden somewhere in them.

"No, no thanks. Well . . ."

"Yes, of course, you must be going, mustn't you? We've held you up quite unconscionably already. Shame on us. Well, perhaps we'll meet again." She extended her hand for the second time, her bracelets clattering. One was ivory and the other silver. The sensation of having known her before was even greater with her hand in mine. Our eyes met and held. What was the joke we were sharing?

"You never can tell," I said.

"I'd like it if we did," Jessica Gage said.

She waved after me through the window when I left the store. I bounded up the stairs two at a time on legs that were no longer heavy as stone but bouncy as a sixteen-year-old's rubber ball.

My place looked like Montgomery Street on December 31st when the office drones tore up their calendar books from the played-out year and tossed them out the windows—those windows that weren't hermetically sealed. Whoever had ransacked my stuff had only been interested in my files, such as they were: cardboard boxes organized in ways that had nothing to do with either chronology or the alphabet. Somebody had gone through them in haste, overturning the boxes and scattering years of stories and notes, correspondence and memorabilia into confused heaps.

I went right to the closet. The Walther was still there beside the baseball glove, as was Yollo's address book. It seemed they had only been interested in finding something they thought I had written or was writing. My first thought was the two punks I had spanked and sent packing, but no, they hadn't had time enough and if it had been them the wreckage wouldn't have been restricted to my files. Who then? Who wanted to know what I might be writing? Pressix? Not likely; he would have started by asking me what he should know. Wallach? No, our cards were on the table and he could be pretty certain I wasn't after him. That left one other possibility, or two really, acting as one. Somewhere deep inside me a soft, sad place finally began to turn rigid.

21

The M&M was not dim by design, the way Alfred's was, to create atmosphere. The bar just down Fifth Street from the newspapers was in fact illuminated by five naked light bulbs, but the bulbs no sooner got screwed in than they became weary. The lighting at the M&M was a perfect complement to its out-of-date calendars and its faded aquamarine walls. Here and there the aqua was chipped away to reveal a coat of yellow beneath it and orange beneath that covering a gray-white and below that an even earlier coat of aqua.

Nobody was drinking except for a couple of printers wearing the blocked newsprint hats that were the trademark of their endangered species, an old lady with two shopping bags beside her stool and a tawny cat curled up on the scarred bar beside her boilermaker, and a rewrite man from *The Bulletin* who I knew by sight but not by name. We traded nods. I took a seat on the far rim of the horseshoe bar to discourage conversation.

Aretha arrived wearing a white satin evening dress.

"Evening, Miss Palladine," said the bartender.

"You didn't have to put on the dog just to meet me, Reeth," I said.

"Henry, until you've written twenty-two grafs on deadline about the dullest ball in the history of mankind while wearing a nine-hundred-dollar Cerucci don't give me any guff, okay?''

"I can't help it, guff's my middle name.''

"You've been funnier, Big Stuff.''

"The truth is I don't feel funny tonight. It just isn't a funny night. Is it, Mother?'' I said in the direction of the bag lady. When she didn't acknowledge me I motioned to the bartender to give her another round. He put a shot glass of well whiskey in front of her and drew a fresh draft and leaned over to say something, looking in my direction.

"It isn't a funny night, is it, Mother?''

Very solemnly she nodded. She continued to nod and then took a dainty sip of her whiskey and a long swallow of beer, wiping her lips with the back of a hand. Her nails were long and yellow, broken at the tops.

"Well, Henry, how's your story coming?''

"I'm not writing a story, Aretha. Why does everybody insist that I'm writing a story? You know, somebody ransacked my place looking for what they thought I was writing.''

"Well, Henry, count your blessings, we don't all have such devoted followings. Who cared that much about your deathless prose?''

"I've got an idea it was my former employer and, uh, somebody else.''

"Oh, Henry, you aren't still hung up on that, are you, baby? Richard the Second a cat burglar—you can't be serious?''

"Well, whoever does that sort of thing for him. And I am serious, he's playing some kind of cat and mouse game with me.''

"If you ask me, you're paranoid. You really should get a grip on yourself or you're going to do more harm to yourself than he ever did. Why don't you sue him for firing you? It would make you feel better.''

"Courts don't award the kind of compensation I'm interested in exacting.'' It came out sounding sullen, but I wasn't going to tell Aretha all that I knew or suspected.

"Henry, don't self-destruct. Please.''

"Aretha, I . . . self-destruct? 'Careless, reckless, a disgrace,' it's become a kind of trinity of self-abuse ever since he told me that's what he thought of me, had Mazer tell me. There are times I go back over my life with a microscope and it scares me half to death thinking that he might be right. But he isn't. He thinks his money and his power and his newspaper have bought him a grant of immunity from a higher authority. And maybe they have, but the time is coming when I'm going to have him down in the gutter with me, and then we'll see."

"Baby, listen to me. If you let him consume you, he's won. Do you hear what I'm saying?"

"Yeah, but if I don't see this through to the end then I've lost, and that's a lot worse. But what was that message about, that you may have found out something important?"

"Okay," she said. She sipped her drink and I mine and we both let the atmosphere ease up. "Well, I thought it was all over when they arrested those two insects who murdered Harry. I had picked up something I thought would interest you and then I just entirely forgot about it, you know. But then I heard that the flyboy, Jerry Cole, had been killed too and I thought, ah-ha, this is as Byzantine as a seating arrangement at one of Charlotte Maillard's intimate little soirees for three dozen and maybe Henry'd want to hear about what little Aretha dug up anyhoo."

"That's why I'm plying you with liquor."

"You do take me to the swellest places, Henry. Which reminds me, how's your little tart at that dump on Geary Street?"

"Day old, Reeth. Forget it."

She arched her penciled eyebrows and made a little tsk-tsk sound with her valentine lips. "If you let me bum a cigarette, Lady Killer, I'll tell you *everything*."

I reached into my pocket and pulled out my cigarettes but the packet was empty. "All I've got is a little cigar. I'll buy us a pack, what kind do you want?"

"That's okay," she said. "I'll smoke the cigar."

"You will?"

"Don't look so shocked. Why not?"

"Oh, hell, Aretha, you know why not."

"Give me the goddamn cigar. Anyway, it looks like a cigarillo. You ain't half as macho as you want me to believe."

"These are *not* some kind of stunted Shermans, Aretha. These are real cigars. Like pygmies are real Africans."

She put the cigar between her bright red lips and waited for me to light it. I held a match up while she drew on it until it was burning. She puffed on it for a minute and then offered it to me. "Want a drag?"

"You don't drag on a cigar. You puff it."

She put the cigar back in her mouth. "Okay. Are you ready for the scoop?"

"Shoot."

"Remember when that delightful girl was slopping my coffee, that night, you asked me what I knew about Ricky Thiesmann and Harry? And I said there had been rumors? Well, Aretha's been asking some discreet questions and there's a whole wheelbarrow-full more to it than just rumors."

"I'll say."

"You already know about this?"

"It depends. Go ahead."

"Well, what I hear is that there's a long incestuous relationship between the two families. I think Harry *was* gay. Maybe that accounts for why his wife left him after their daughter was born and why he never remarried. You know how he liked to squire beautiful women half his age? I mean, that can be read more than one way, don't you think? Anyhoo, it's his wife that's the point. Or a part of the point. I'm told she was a very beautiful girl, good genes, good bank references. The way I hear it, and we're going back a long way here, Thiesmann loved the same girl. They both proposed and she chose Harry. Joke's on her. By the time she wakes up to the fact that she's made what you might call a sinful error, Thiesmann's married on the rebound. Have you ever seen *his* wife? A rebound type of allure if I ever saw such a thing. She's about as warm as her second-best china. They say the marriage is conducted with all the intimacy of arms-control negotiations.

"You with me so far? Okay, well, the scoop is that Thiesmann and Harry's missus, Vicki Cavanaugh, that was her maiden name, had an affair that was hotter than 1906. No real secret about it. This is just about the time that Harry's beginning to make a name for himself with his column and Thiesmann's taking over *The Courier* from his daddy. Birth control being what it was back then, Vicki gets herself in a delicate way. Now, of course, Harry knows it's not *his*, Thiesmann's got to be the papa. What happened next is a little unclear. From what I hear Harry put some awful slur on Olivia Thiesmann into his column, into her husband's newspaper. Harry was still at *The Courier* then. Can you imagine? I mean, what's the point of owning your own newspaper if your gossip columnist can insult your wife in it?

"Thiesmann confronts Harry. In the lower bar at The Mark, is the way it was told to me. Decks him, pow! Right in front of everybody. But doesn't fire him. Isn't that exquisite? Keeps him on the payroll, oooh, delicious. This cigar stinks, Henry. Why didn't you warn me it wasn't a ladylike cigarillo?"

"My oversight, Reeth. Don't lose your place." I went to the cigarette machine and bought us a pack. Aretha had ordered a fresh round. "You know what? Your story proves what I was telling you. Thiesmann's perfectly capable of playing a game of psychological torment." I didn't add: when his family's involved.

"Forget that, will you? You like Aretha's story so far?"

"Yeah, I do."

"Okay. Well, Harry had his pride even if it took him a few months to find it. He quits. Crosses over to *The Bulletin* and there he remains ever since, the undisputed monarch of San Francisco journalism. Vicki meanwhile has the child. She's figuring on a divorce. Maybe two divorces. But Thiesmann has cooled on it. They say *his* father issued an ultimatum, either the newspaper or else Vicki and his illegitimate offspring. Thiesmann *fils* chooses *The Courier* and the burdensome Olivia, power before poontang, a message not lost on us girls. Vicki is distraught, she splits for Europe and dies there. Suicide, naturally, is whispered about.''

"So that means that Judy Shugart really *is* Thiesmann's daughter."

"You know her?" Aretha sounded surprised.

"No, not really. Seen her once or twice is all."

Aretha arched a penciled eyebrow. "What's the blood in the cheeks then, just natural high spirits?''

"Your presence so close by, Aretha, it always has this blood boiling effect.''

"Oh, yeah?''

"Scout's honor.''

Aretha looked at her watch. "Yoicks! Time to put this girl to bed. So what do you think about all that?''

"I think it's a good yarn, and from other things I know, probably true.''

"Call me a taxi, Henry, you've got connections. Unless you want to come home with me?''

"I would love that, Reeth, I really would. But it's my time of the month.''

She struck a pose, both hands on her hips and her head cocked, and I went to the pay phone and dialed Checker Cab. While the line was ringing I remembered that I was due to go back to work the next night. For a few days there I had forgotten that there was more to life than a story I wasn't writing.

22

It was something of a relief to be back behind the wheel where all questions had answers that could be calculated in twenty-cent increments every time the meter clicked. A convention of thirty thousand chiropractors was in town being driven from Union Square to Fisherman's Wharf, from Trader Vic's to the Top of the Mark by a thousand taxi drivers with aching lower backs. The money they threw our way was a balm for a multitude of pains. Something I felt sure Al would understand. I had never met Al, who was the author of a graffito I drove by during the night. Somebody before Al had spray painted this message on the side of a building:

> SUPPORT BLACK STRUGGLE
> FOR HUMAN RIGHTS

Along came Al, no doubt in his cups, to draw a slash through Black:

> AL'S
> SUPPORT ~~BLACK~~ STRUGGLE
> FOR HUMAN RIGHTS

Al was an artist; he particularized the general and his particular plaint was universal.

Tuesday morning I poured myself a cup of starter fluid

and brought Yollo's address book and the shiny new Walther with me to the table. Slowly and cautiously I inserted a full clip and sighted along the barrel toward Carol Doda's mammillary excesses. Pyoo, pyoo, take that, you bastards.

Poor fat Yollo with his skunk's beard would be a sight in angel wings. Did they serve their eggs with the whites crisp and the yolks runny at the Big Kitchen in the Sky? All his considerable instinct for survival had not been enough to preserve him against the murderous indifference of the bad people who wanted what he had in his satchel and thought killing him might enable them to get away with their own mistakes. A victim of circumstance, a fall guy. I started looking through his address book trying again to decipher his system of cryptic abbreviations and finally found what I expected to find but hoped not to. After Yollo, Jerry Cole had been eliminated for reasons I was only beginning to understand.

I cradled the Walther in both my hands. When Thiesmann had gone to face Harry Shugart on the night they declared open season on the town gossip, he had taken a gun with him to avenge his son. But I had snatched Ricky and frightened him into telling me things his father didn't want anybody to know, and all he had done was set his minions to spying on me. But of course he could afford to bide his time because Judy had given him a direct line into what I was thinking, into how things could come unraveled for them. Or so he had every reason to believe.

Wallach had said that Judy put out a contract on Cole. Did that jibe with what I had seen in her living room? It could. The distress of loss is hard to distinguish from other kinds of distress, especially if you're seeing it through a closed window peeping through the slats in a shutter. Maybe she felt awful about what she had done. It wasn't entirely clear yet.

I saw her then, crossing Broadway from the north, coming toward my front door. She had on oversize dark glasses that made her look like a movie star trying to hide her identity because the sun was hidden behind a late lifting fog and the day was a silky gray. I hurriedly put the gun and Yollo's little book away and unlatched the door before I sat back down with the sports section, propping my feet across the corner of the table.

"It's open," I shouted when she knocked.

She rushed over to me and sank onto her knees, burying her face low on my chest. My hand had a life of its own, it stroked her golden hair while I stared blankly out of the skylight. She smelled as good as ever and I responded to the soft pressure of her face against my midriff. Finally she looked up.

"It just stinks, doesn't it, Jones? I never expected it to be fair but I didn't expect everybody to keep getting killed." A tear rolled out from under her shades. "You're not going to get murdered too, are you?"

"No."

"Promise."

"I swear on my collection of major league autographs." I wanted to be hard but I was merely a man, a man who was grateful that some long frozen places were painfully thawing.

"*You* collect autographs?"

"No."

She smiled, a wan smile.

"That's better."

"Love and death," she said. "Love and death and the whole damn ball of Weltschmerz."

"You took the word right out of my mouth, except I can't pronounce it."

"That's because your father never took you to Heidelberg for your summer holiday."

I didn't ask which father she meant. "Did yours?"

"No." She began to cry again. "Do you know what I need?" Her face was buried against me again.

"Breakfast."

"To be held, Jones. Tight. All over." I could feel her lips moving through my thin shirt, and her warm breath. Something was going on here and Mr. Jones was finally beginning to understand what. The knowledge was scant comfort for the disappointment.

With a silent groan I took her by the shoulders and eased her off me. "Breakfast is a better idea, believe me. Mother Henry knows. We can talk."

She let me guide her to her feet. "Talk doesn't touch it."

"There's a lot to talk about."

"You mean us, Jones? Or all the horrible stuff? I'm sick of the horrible stuff. But I'll do whatever you say because I love you." She kissed me. Her lips were warm and salty from her tears and petal soft. It would have been nice to believe she meant it. I grabbed my chamois jacket off the back of a chair and led the way out.

On the street she linked her arm through mine. We walked slowly, not talking. Men we passed kept turning around to look after her. The cafe was empty except for the lady behind the counter reading an Italian-language newspaper. We took a table by a window that faced Washington Square Park. She ordered a double espresso. So did I.

"I thought you said breakfast?"

"This is breakfast. You're not hungry, are you?"

"Oh, Jonesy, you're really wonderful, you know that?"

I lit her cigarette. "Judy, why was Jerry Cole killed?" She had said to me once that Cole was a useful man. It had seemed at the time a peculiar turn of phrase for a romantic girl.

"I keep going over it in my mind. It has to involve all that stuff that happened the night Harry was murdered, doesn't it? I mean, Frimmer and Pendleton were Jerry's men. If they murdered Harry then Jerry was behind it, right? But I always end up going around in circles. Tell me what you think."

"Maybe Cole knew too many things that threatened other people. I suppose he wasn't useful anymore, or more useful dead than alive to whoever wanted him killed."

"But who?"

"You told me Jerry wanted you to collect the coke Yollo

was delivering the night Harry Shugart was killed. But that isn't exactly the way it happened. Frimmer and Pendleton were there because Jer-baby was planning to rip off a delivery, the delivery Yollo was making. But the whole night was a series of botch ups. Later on Jerry and his thugs caught up with Yollo and killed him and took the coke after all. But because the coke hadn't been delivered and paid for it still really belonged to the people Yollo was working for—he was just a middleman—and they wanted it back. In fact, they got it from Frimmer and Pendleton before the police caught them.''

"They *did*? How do you know all this, Jones?''

"By the way, when did you and Jerry get engaged?''

"In May. But why?''

"Anyway, after his bozos were arrested Jerry went on the lam.'' As casually as I could I asked, "Where did he tell you he was headed?'' Deep inside I was still hoping to be wrong.

Too glibly she said, "He just said he had to go down south for a while until the heat was off. So is that what you think happened, these people Yollo Current was working for found him and killed him?''

"You want another espresso?''

She shook her head and smiled at me. She still was wearing her dark glasses. "A latte. I'm gonna OD on caffeine.'' I told the lady reading the newspaper what we wanted and we both watched her as she made the new drinks. Judy lit another Gauloise and we remained silent until the steaming cups were on the table and the lady had returned to her perch at the back of the cafe. Our tabletop was a checked blue Formica, faded with use and age. I smiled reassuringly at Judy, who reached out and stroked the back of my hand.

"These people who supplied Yollo Current, the ones you think killed Jerry, who are they?''

"Oh, they didn't do Jerry. I thought so for a while but I was wrong.''

"No? But I thought you said—well, I'm just a scatterbrain. Who was it?''

"Probably some button men, some other interchangeable parts like Frimmer and Pendleton. The question is, who hired them? And the answer is, whoever had found Cole useful alive and now saw that if he died under the right circumstances he would be even more useful."

"Jones, do the police know all this stuff you're telling me?"

"Most of it."

"Well? When are you going to stop teasing me and tell me who it was?"

"The person behind it is somebody the cops are afraid to touch without absolute proof, and even then they'd act only if they were afraid it would get out that they hadn't. It's got to be your father."

Her lovely head moved abruptly sideways, as if it had been slapped. "That's a creepy fucking thing to say. What's got into you?"

"I don't mean Shugart, Judy."

She ran her red nails over her palms, as if she were trying to clutch something that wasn't there. She didn't speak at once. I waited. Finally she sighed and took off her dark glasses and looked straight at me. Her eyes were so blue it hurt to look directly into them. I had never seen her so serious or so beautiful. "How long have you known?"

"A few days. The thing is, I wish you hadn't lied to me about so much."

"I lie to men without even thinking about it, Jones, that's just the way it is. But I haven't been lying about how I feel about you. I don't want you to think that because— well, because I just don't want you to. This hasn't been simple for me, or easy. I'm only twenty-two years old."

"How old were you when your mother died?"

"Six. I barely knew her. The last few years of her life she was in institutions mostly and I was kept in boarding schools. I've always thought I hated her, because she was weak, because she deserted me. Until—until recently. Harry refused to talk about her and I was so angry and I guess scared that I was to blame that I never asked him what had happened straight out. Oh, Jonesy, I wish it weren't this way. If . . .''

"The saddest word in the language. You know, the very first time we met you started to say that Thiesmann had told you about me but you stopped yourself. I didn't catch it then but later I understood. And then when you told me I was probably dangerous, you meant to you and Thiesmann, to your father. So the two of you decided you would keep an eye on me.''

Her look was level. "You still don't see it all, do you? It's not that simple, Jones, not for me.''

"When did you find out he was your father?''

"Valentine's Day, can you believe it?'' she said bitterly.

"How did he persuade you?''

"Letters, he had letters from my mom. The poor woman was crazy about him. You see, he had started to suspect—well, it really doesn't matter what—something that isn't so bad but that he thought was just awful and he couldn't talk to anyone about it, it was like a family disgrace. It made him want to let me know I was his daughter. He wanted my sympathy,'' she said acidly.

"You mean about Ricky?''

"You know about that?''

"Nobody's told you about my little chat with Ricky?''

"No, my f— Dick doesn't want Ricky to know about me.''

"So he wanted to take you away from Shugart. That's a hell of a reason for letting you know you were his daughter twenty years too late.''

"It's about as weird as it gets talking to you about this stuff. Do you know what I mean? Is there anything you don't know about us, Jones?''

"I don't know if it was you or Jer-baby who tipped the police about Yollo. Him, I suppose, to deflect attention away from Frimmer and Pendleton. But it could have been you. I don't know for sure why you decided to become engaged to Cole a few months after Thiesmann persuaded you you were his daughter, but I suppose you thought Jer-baby was malleable enough to help you bring down Thiesmann somehow for all he had done, or hadn't done, and it was useful to have Cole thinking you were all his. But then the night Shugart died everything began to change, didn't it? And I came stumbling into the picture shooting off my mouth about how Thiesmann had done me dirty and I was going to get my revenge.''

She smiled. ''I told you I wanted you for a knight errant.''

''You should have been named Guinevere. I don't know either, not for a certainty, that you were the one to put the contract out on Cole. God knows you had reason to once you knew Frimmer and Pendleton had killed Harry. It made it clear to you what had really been going down that night. There are people who say it was your contract.''

''And you believe them?'' She seemed stunned and hurt but the pucker in her throat was palpitating.

I didn't answer at once. Sunlight was just penetrating the thinning fog, making a gauzy, radiant light. In the park a stout woman was walking her dog and an old Chinese man in a pajamalike costume was moving with infinite patience through the t'ai chi positions. ''I feel old,'' I said.

She flushed and put her glasses back on. ''If you believe *that*,'' she said in a tone I had never heard her use before, a tone as final as an auctioneer's hammer, ''you are old. You are yesterday.'' When she left the cafe the flimsy glass door slammed behind her.

''You want 'other espress?''

I shook my head.

''Young people, they got hot heads. High-a spirits. Is a bellissima young lady. You amora?''

''No.'' In my mind I was itemizing the things, large and small, I had never told Judy. I hadn't ever told her that it was my taxi that she had called the night Harry Shugart died. Nor that Jerry Cole's name wasn't anywhere to be found in Yollo's little book, but hers was. Under B, for Blondie, and the address 3670-side. Where Yollo and I had both had our no-gos. Wallach had been telling the truth, it had been her deal. Cole had sent his thugs to rip off the coke from her, maybe even to kill her, I wouldn't have put it past him, and on the evidence Judy wouldn't have either. They didn't find her or the coke because, fortunately for her and unfortunately for Harry Shugart, she had been late. Like always. But when she found out that it was Frimmer and Pendleton who had killed Harry, evidently when they blundered upon him that night while they were looking for the cocaine, she had understood what Cole had intended. Suddenly everything had fallen into place for her. She revised her script to snare both her betrayers, Thiesmann and Cole, in the same net. And left the rest to her perfectly cast Lancelot.

"You go after-a her?"

I was glad for Judy's sake she had a running head start on all that would be pursuing her. "It wouldn't do any good. No, I think I'll have to talk with her father about it."

~~~~ 23 ~~~~~~~~~~~~~~~~~~~~~

I arrived at the employees' entrance of *The Courier* at a few minutes before seven the next morning without having slept and made a point of saying good morning to Charlie Bates, who was in charge of building security. I was wearing my best gray suit and a black knit tie that had been Buddy's, which I had taken from his wardrobe but never put on before.

"Hey. Long time no see," Charlie said.

"Smells just as bad as always in here."

Charlie guffawed. "You're awful early."

"First day back on the job, gotta catch the worm."

Charlie nodded sagely. "Right," he said.

I avoided the elevator because I didn't want to be seen by anybody less gullible than Charlie. The stairs to the top floor let me out in the reception room outside Thiesmann's office. His secretary wouldn't be arriving until 8:30 and I hoped that would be enough time to get ready.

I went directly into Thiesmann's spacious office and put my briefcase down on his desk. There was a Persian throw rug under the desk. The briefcase contained the Walther, a high quality three hour cassette tape, copper wire, a small tool pouch that Yollo had once given me as a Christmas present, and a tape recorder in case I needed it, but I didn't think I would. I removed the tools and the wire.

167

The door connecting Thiesmann's office to his secretary's was ajar and I went back and shut it.

What I was looking for was easy to find. I picked up the telephone console and traced the line that led through a tiny hole drilled in the top of the teak desk into the right hand top drawer. Sure enough, there was a tape recorder in there. The love of power is the love of self. A man with Thiesmann's narcissism would want a record of what he had said, and what had been said to him. The Nixon syndrome.

I played around with some of the buttons on the telephone console until I found the one that triggered the tape. The reels began to turn noiselessly. I was grateful that he had equipped himself with a high-quality machine. Out loud I said, "One two three four I hope nobody walks through the door. Five six seven eight behind me they'll slam the gate." I rewound and played it back. Nothing but the slither and hum of the tape itself. It hadn't worked. I tried it again with the same result. I punched the button to stop the tape. Evidently the phone had to be off the cradle for the machine to record. What I had to do was rig it so that the apparatus was live even when the phone was on the hook.

I sat down in Thiesmann's deeply padded swivel desk chair and turned over the console. Then I opened my tool pouch and with a small screwdriver removed the plate from the bottom of the console. I was staring at the twisted clumps of multicolored wiring inside the instrument when there was a sudden noise behind me. My heart raced and my skin turned prickly. The clock on the wall was striking the quarter hour. Slowly my body relaxed, absorbing the message from my brain that everything was still okay. I took a deep breath and went back to examining the wiring, cursing myself for not having paid more attention to the things Yollo had shown me. He would have looked at this setup, muttered his contempt, and dug in there with those breakfast sausage fingers of his. I was cursed with my own wide peasant fingers. I interlaced them and cracked my knuckles.

One at a time I began to pick loose the wires and follow them from terminal to terminal. When the clock was striking half past seven I found the one I thought connected the tape line to the telephone and sent the impulse that activated the recorder. It would have been easier if it had been set up like an ordinary answering machine, but it wasn't. Thiesmann had to push a button when he wanted to begin recording. And the phone had to be off the cradle. First I had to rewire it so it would record with the phone still in place. After that I had another problem. I kept experimenting. A few minutes after eight, with sweat trickling down my rib cage, I thought I finally had it right. Once more I started the tape rolling. "One two three four please Lord no time for more." I rewound the machine and hit the play button. My own voice began to recite. "One, two . . ." I stopped the machine.

The mechanical difficulties had been disposed of, but now my problem was timing. Once Thiesmann was in his office I couldn't just go over to his desk and push a button. I had to record without his knowledge. But his secretary arrived punctually at 8:30 and he didn't usually show up until some time after 9:30. The tape would record for only ninety minutes on one side. I hadn't been able to find a longer-playing cassette than that. If I triggered it before the secretary came to work and he was a few minutes late I would have maybe twenty minutes left on the tape in which to get him to say the things I wanted him to say, and that wasn't enough.

I sat there considering how to handle this, drumming my fingers on the desk. It seemed insurmountable. Minutes passed. The clock struck 8:15 and I still didn't know. The secretary was due in fifteen minutes. My fingers were beating their tattoo on a leather covered appointment book that matched the pen stand and the blotter. Idly I opened it and turned the pages. I looked at Thiesmann's schedule for the morning. His first appointment was at nine o'clock with Goldman, the company controller, to discuss the annual report.

Moving fast now I rescrewed the plate to the bottom of

the console. The minutes were passing with berserk haste. I righted the console and put it back in place. I repacked the tools and the wire into my briefcase. The tape in his machine I replaced with my own. At 8:25 I depressed the record button and watched the little red light come on and the tape begin to spin slowly from one spool to the other. I shut the desk drawer very gently.

· There was a large closet in which he kept some changes of clothes and a wet bar, and that was where I planned to hide until he showed up. I stepped toward it and turned the knob. It was 8:28. The closet was locked. Why? I mean why keep the office wide open and lock the closet? Had the cleaning ladies been at the booze?

I could hear voices and footsteps. People were arriving to begin the day's work. I went into my wallet and brought out a plastic card and slipped it into the lock. As I dropped it into my pocket I noticed it was a telephone company credit card issued to the *San Francisco Courier*. I closed the closet door behind me just as his secretary was beginning to open the door to the office, and breathed a huge sigh of relief that I muffled as best I could by burying my mouth in the shoulder of one of his dinner jackets.

24

I was suddenly blind. I stood absolutely still waiting for my breathing to return to normal and my eyes to adjust. A few more minutes now and there would be nothing and nobody separating us.

His secretary came into the office, her heels clicking across the floor until she reached the Persian rug. She was doing something near Thiesmann's desk because I heard the chair squeak. Had I left any sign of my presence? Was she examining the room, suspecting an intruder? Would she call for help and would I be dragged out of the closet like a lurking maniac with a gun in his briefcase? I held my breath. My stomach, already clenched with anticipation, seemed to push up against my spine. After what seemed like many minutes I heard her crossing the floor again on her way out. My mouth was dry. I put my ear against the door hoping to hear if she was making a phone call or summoning Charlie Bates, but I couldn't hear a thing. No news is good news. Not true. In the newspaper business no news was bad news; bad news was good news. I was bad news, for Thiesmann I hoped, but just possibly for myself. Was what I was staging here the final act in a drama of self-wreckage? I wanted to believe I was doing this because justice demanded that he be held accountable like anybody else, but would I have come this far if he hadn't stuck his barbs into the very place in my psyche I most feared about myself? Maybe my problem was that even when what was demanded was action I was still asking questions. Hurry up, hurry up, Thiesmann, the longer I wait the more my certainty wavers.

Finally I heard the secretary again, she was saying something but I couldn't make out what. Then I heard her more distinctly. ". . . . at nine, it's all there on your desk."

It was startling to hear him say from very close to the closet, "That's fine, Dorothy. I'll have my coffee now." Was he going to hang up his jacket? I was poised but nothing happened except that she left the room. When she came back I heard the clinks of cups and saucers and spoons from near his desk.

"Will there be anything else, Mr. Thiesmann?"

"Send Goldman directly in when he arrives." The connecting door between his office and hers shut and he was alone, we were alone. I felt a savage excitement as I turned the knob and stepped into his office. The bright light flooding the windows behind him assaulted my vision so all I saw was a dark silhouette awash in rays of sunlight. Black spots danced in the distance between us.

He said, "Good morning, Ben." Unflappable bastard.

He began to come into focus in front of an open window, his newspaper held in one hand, his reading glasses perched on his long patrician nose. He was standing sideways to me, looking at me past his left shoulder.

"Is there something I can do for you?" He sounded very nearly disinterested and entirely in command of himself and the situation. That wasn't the way I had planned it.

"Why don't you tell your secretary to put off Goldman? What we're going to talk about is going to take a while." My voice sounded detached to me, as if it had a life of its own.

"I could as easily tell her to call the police." His free hand was poised above the telephone. I studied him the way you look at somebody you've just realized you love, as if I'd never noticed him before, conscious of details like the mole on his left cheek. But this was not love I felt.

"Then you won't find out what I know. And you want to know." I was the one who had to know, that was what had brought me all this way. I waited to see if he cared as much as I did.

He considered that for a moment before he pushed the intercom button. He sat down in his chair. "Dorothy, something's come up that requires my attention. Tell Goldman he'll hear from us when I'm free." He clicked her off in the middle of her saying, "Yes, Mr.—"

He extended a hand toward a leather wing chair, one of two facing him across his desk, a confident gesture. I took the seat and put the briefcase at my side. He watched me without any show of emotion or reaction, peering at me over the top of his glasses. He had a high forehead and iron-gray hair that was cut close to his scalp and lay flat, Caesar-like. His jawline was long and straight and his chin smallish and rounded. He had the lean, rangy body of a tennis player and wore his clothes with an ease that only the very rich and certain black men have, as if the suit were not merely covering or adornment but an extension of himself. I recognized his Nordic blue eyes; they were Judy's eyes. The left one was narrower than the right, shrewder, more observant. He removed his half-frame reading spectacles with long, elegant, strong fingers and placed them carefully on his leather desk blotter next to his coffee cup.

"I'm waiting." His tone was nearly ironic.

"Where do we start?" My words still sounded remote and too loud. "How about the night you rushed over to Shugart's house to redeem Ricky's honor? You took a gun with you."

It was calculated to break down his commanding pose, and it seemed to work. Some of the healthy color drained out of his cheeks and little puckers formed just below the bones. Go ahead, you bastard, feel the loathing.

"Why in the world should I discuss that with you?"

"Because you can."

He swiveled in his chair, turning his profile toward me. "I took the gun to scare him. It wasn't loaded, as a matter of fact. I think I intended to shove it in his mouth and make him beg for his life. He was a contemptuous weakling and what he had done to my son he had done to get at me.'' He shot me a sharp look but his eyes were clouded over with a hatred that included Shugart, me, and if I didn't miss my guess, himself for having the son he did. I felt sorry for Ricky. "Do you have children? You don't, do you? No. I knew why he had done it.''

"To get even because of Judy, because of you and Judy's mother?''

"Yes.'' He said it quietly, making a pyramid of his long fingers. "Yes. Judy. I'm pleased you've come here like this because you're going to pay for the things you did to my son, for . . . You're leaving here in police custody, you're finished.''

"And?''

"And? Oh. I was too late. Those hoodlums who worked for Jerry Cole had beaten me to him.'' He laughed, a deprecating laugh. "When I saw Harry dead I felt great regret. I would never have the opportunity to humiliate him again. Humiliating Harry seems to have taken up a disproportionate amount of my life.''

"Was Ricky the first time he ever got in his licks?''

"In many years, yes. In many years.''

"After I had my talk with Ricky, why didn't you come after me? Or send someone? The cops or the thugs, it hardly matters to you, does it?''

I had never been looked at with such loathing as was distorting his face then. "I was persuaded to wait.''

"Judy convinced you it was a good thing to let me be because whatever I found out she could get out of me, and that way the two of you would know what information was available that might jeopardize her.''

"From the time you worked for me, I always knew that you would self-destruct, y'see?'' He made a palms up gesture to indicate that was what was happening now.

"Why did you fire me, Thiesmann?''

He smiled bitterly and began to swivel in his chair, left to right, left to right. "Mazer told you at the time. You are a disgrace to our profession, an assassin not a reporter, a purveyor—''

''Yeah, I remember all that.'' My teeth were clenched and I was breathing through my nose. ''I've never forgotten a word of it. Maybe I wasn't meant to be a reporter.'' I hadn't known I thought that; it shocked me but I couldn't stop to consider it now. ''But why did you fire me when you did?''

''You were out of control, and that made you dangerous, dangerous to *The Courier*, thrashing around trying to 'get the goods' as you would have it, 'get the goods' on somebody in the establishment. Somebody, anybody, with power and authority and responsibility. You think power is some kind of bullying privilege because you are a very immature man who has never known real responsibility. But power is a matter of responsibility, of responsibility for—''

''Save it for commencement speeches, Thiesmann. What's more likely is that somebody had their screws into you. Probably the same cops I was after. Did they use Judy against you? *They* knew she was your daughter, it was probably buried in a twenty-year-old intelligence file, the kind of stuff they keep on you and people like you just in case it'll come in handy someday. What did they do, tell you how much of a pity it would be if they had to bust the girl for dealing coke? Did they play on your guilt? Maybe it was Judy, or maybe it was something else, but I can just imagine the way it went: 'We've both got a problem here, Mr. Thiesmann. But, hey, listen, we're reasonable people. Why don't you just shitcan Henry and get him off our backs and we'll forget about this unfortunate incident in your past and both our problems will be solved.' ''

''Is that an example of your investigative reporting? I'd like to know how you can prove it, not that the facts have ever interfered with your 'getting' someone before. I know all about you, Henry, all about your arrogance. I tried to teach you a lesson, that this information you were gathering, this proof of corruption as you called it, was available to you only because of the authority of *The Courier*. Without *The Courier* you're nothing. A taxi driver,'' he said with a dismissive wave of his long, graceful hand. ''Arrogant nobodies like you have been telling me how to exercise my power all my life. You don't really think for a moment that I pay the slightest attention, do you?''

''You didn't even have the guts to fire me yourself.''

''Why in the world should I have?''

''You know, Thiesmann, you're ashamed of your son and your daughter was born to another man's wife and it took you twenty years to acknowledge her. And yet you sit here handing out this pious crap about power and responsibility. You were perfectly willing to barge into Judy's world, imperfect as it may have been, and completely wreck it because you were licking your wounds about Ricky. You were willing to fire me, too, because the kind of reporting I was doing jeopardized you and your paper because you're part and parcel of all the stink in this town. Of course what you did to Judy and what you did to me, that's merely selfish. All it shows is that you're too vain and too certain of your privilege to consider the effects of your actions on their victims. But Jerry Cole, that's something else, isn't it? I mean, that's a pretty steep price to pay to make the girl love you. Having a man killed.''

''What you're talking about now is something you could never understand. Never. Jerry Cole was trying to blackmail me, extort money from me to protect Judy. He said she had been the one to hire the men they arrested for killing Harry.''

We were suspended in a world out of time, the two of us alone on a barren, burned plain, our mouths dry with the ashes of hatred.

''And Judy admitted it to you, right? And asked for your help? In fact, it was she who brought the note from Cole after he went into hiding, wasn't it? You sap.''

He made no response. Just drilled his eyes into mine.

''Sure, your Goldilocks showed you the note and said, please save me, Daddy. We can't go to the police because it's all true. Get rid of that nasty man before it's too late for me. And you, you saw your chance to make up for all those years of compounding your broken promises to her mother, your mean betrayals. It only took a spot of murder.

"The only thing is, it wasn't like Judy told you at all. What your dear little daughter's done is taken her revenge for Vicki. Judy wasn't the one who had Shugart and Yollo Current killed, that was Cole's work. So the blackmail message couldn't possibly have been legitimate, it was Judy's trap for you. You see, she understood you a lot better than you understood her. She knew that now that you had finally acknowledged her as your daughter you wouldn't want her marrying a polished thug, a nobody like Jerry Cole. We all know how you feel about nobodies, Dick." He winced when I used his Christian name.

"She knew it would be a relief to you to have Cole out of the picture, and she gave you a reason to have it done. Something you could arrange for her that would really suit you too. So she played on your weakness, the weakness she understood perfectly, the same vanity and selfish sense of self-worth that caused her mother and then her so much pain. She understood that you had told her the truth only because you were bitterly disappointed and vengeful when you found out Ricky was sleeping with Harry Shugart. Did you think she'd light up with delight to find she was a Thiesmann? Are you that blinded by your vanity?"

"I'm putting an end to this farce," he said, reaching for the phone.

I talked faster. "The minute you told her that you were her father—picking Valentine's Day was a sweet touch, schmuck—Judy understood that you had killed Vicki as surely as if you had fired a bullet into her. And the life she'd lived had made Judy resourceful. She wasn't about to let you get away with it. She became your grateful little kitten, didn't she? And you accepted it because you thought it was your due. It was an act. By a beautiful young woman who was seducing you into believing she was overjoyed to be your little princess at long last. Well, she's succeeded in taking her mother's revenge, hasn't she? After all these years she's made you show your true nature. You're a murderer, an ordinary garden variety murderer. She's used you and she's used me, too, because she knew I was the only one who hated you as much as she did, and that I would take it all the way to you, wouldn't stop until you were hurt and maybe destroyed, the way you destroyed Vicki. And her.''

Now that my moment had come I felt only pity for the man. Not sympathy, but pity, a low emotion.

''Paying those men Judy found to kill that filthy little blackmailer was *not* the same as killing him myself.'' His words were slurred and his usually firm mouth was wobbly.

I wanted to nail it down, so that he couldn't wriggle free somehow. I wanted every detail on the tape. ''How much did it cost you to have Jerry Cole murdered?''

His left eye, the shrewder eye, narrowed. He stood up abruptly and came around the desk and seized my briefcase. I let him take it. He opened the clasps and looked inside, shaking the contents around to get a closer look. Then he upended the briefcase on his desk, everything including the Walther spilling out onto his copy of *The Courier*, overturning the coffee cup, which made a dark, spreading stain on the leather blotter.

''No tuna sandwich,'' I said. ''Sorry.''

He picked up the coil of copper wire in his long fingers and held it contemplatively. Then he unzipped the leather pouch that held the tools. I sat watching as he went behind his desk again and pulled open the drawer with the tape spinning inside it. When he began to reach for the tape recorder, I stood. He lunged for the Walther, grabbing it in both hands and leveling it at me.

I moved toward him. ''You wouldn't shoot me, Thiesmann. That's not your style. You'd have somebody do it for you, like Mazer fired me, like those hoods killed Cole.''

''You are an intruder,'' he shouted and pulled the trigger. In his fury he had forgotten the safety and I grabbed his wrist and the gun in both my hands before he was able to release the catch. I was surprised by his strength as we struggled for the gun, our faces nearly touching, his strained by effort and loathing into something grotesque, purple, with spittle at the corners of his mouth and his blue eyes bulging. Suddenly my heel caught on the edge of the throw rug behind his desk and I slipped. As I did, I lost my grip on him, and his own mammoth expenditure of rage-inspired momentum carried him past me toward the open window.

There was so much adrenaline flowing that everything seemed to be happening in slow motion. I saw his knee slam against the windowsill and carry him forward over the ledge, suspending him half in and half out of the window. There was enough time to grab him and pull him back. I was right beside him. I didn't move.

Looking like a schoolboy about to launch himself into a swimming pool, he plummeted headfirst down toward Mission Street five stories below, screaming the entire way.

25

Jessica Gage ordered the rack of lamb and I a steak. We both began with oysters on the half shell.

"Tell me," she said. "Why didn't the authorities charge you in Mr. Thiesmann's death?"

"I have a good lawyer. He played the tape for the mayor, the Chief, and Pressix and explained that, naturally, it would be necessary to play it in my defense at the trial." I laughed. "Everybody agreed it was an accidental death."

"You have to be very hard in America, I think."

"Everywhere, I would imagine."

"It may be," she said. "I read the newspaper stories of Mr. Thiesmann's death, mind you. Your presence was never mentioned."

"No," I said. The waiter brought our oysters and we were both silent again waiting for him to leave. "Not even in the official police report," I continued when we were alone again. "Accidental death, lost his footing opening a window. I wonder, you know, if I couldn't have prevented him from falling. No, that's not true. What I mean is, I *could* have caught him and I didn't. I wanted him dead, maybe I even wanted to kill him. You know my father was a failure, in his own eyes, and in mine too, but for different reasons. He seemed to regret everything he had ever done. And he never asked himself why, he just blamed 'them,' the people with power or resolve, the people who run things. The people like Thiesmann. It was the first tenet of my upbringing: 'they' can't be trusted, they won't be happy until their foot is in the back of your neck and your face is in the dirt.''

"I simply cannot attempt to eat one of these," she said, gesturing with her tiny fork over the oysters, "with you watching me."

"I have to look at you to talk about these things. I'm surprising myself talking like this."

"You feel you have to escape your father's legacy?"

"No, not exactly, but I think Thiesmann may have died because I haven't. The things he said about me, they cut so deep because *he* said them and because they are things I dread to think may be true about me. I hated him for himself but also because he was 'them.' "

"Yes, but you see you have a sense of fair play. You always have a view of whether what you're doing is just or not. Sometimes it isn't fair or just, but at least you know that and care about it. That makes you a moral man."

"I'd like to think so."

"And what of Judy Shugart? Will she be arrested?" She looked directly at me and there was something in her face I hadn't seen before, a kind of vulnerability, but more than that, pride.

I put my fork down. My throat was too thick to swallow.

"You loved her a great deal, then?"

"No. I—it's not that, really. It's more what's become of her."

She waited for me to continue.

After a moment I said, "She's gone. Disappeared. I think she might be dead."

"Why? Why do you think that?"

"Wallach. One of his shooters, a guy named Beans who I'm sort of fond of actually, I think Wallach may have had Beans hit her. Wallach gave me an envelope, you see. There was ten thousand dollars inside." I took a long swallow of my beer.

"And if your Mr. Wallach did have her—what's the word, bumped?—"

I laughed and so did she and our eyes met and held. I could not shake the conviction that I knew her, knew her well, which is why I was unexpectedly telling her about this. "Hit," I said.

"Yes, how silly of me, hit. If your Mr. Wallach did have her hit, then won't the police be able to deal with that?"

"Not likely. The cops want the whole thing to go away and stay away. No, if Wallach did decide to off Judy, well, it's that certain things have their own momentum. Evil in particular."

"Oh, evil is so common it's banal. Good is far more interesting. It's much rarer and harder to achieve because it goes against our nature but can only be expressed through our nature. And good is always particular. You threw the cash in his face then?"

"No, I took it."

"For whatever reason?"

"Needed the money. Yollo Current was still on a slab down at the morgue. Nobody had claimed the body. Somebody had to bury him. Yollo thought he had been set up, but really he hadn't. That was just his natural paranoia. The poor fat blob just got himself in the wrong place at precisely the wrong time. Cole and his men wanted him because they wanted the cocaine he still had, and maybe they were afraid he had seen them. And the cops wanted him because they knew he had been on Jackson Street that night after somebody called them—maybe Cole, or maybe Judy, I'm still not sure—and after all, he was a drug dealer and a legitimate suspect. I bought him a plot and a nice headstone next to a man who had looked after him, a friend of mine who was murdered too."

"Ah," she said. "This is the first time I've ever eaten oysters and discussed a corpse. Corpses."

"This guy Buddy, he used to call me Sleuth. He said it was because I always wanted to get to the bottom of things.

I've been thinking lately that the name had a kind of premonitory power.''

"Mind you, it is man's business to name things.''

"That's much more difficult than it sounds. I mean calling a chair a chair is easy enough, but naming the self, or love, or anguish, those require all our courage.''

"I write novels in order to name things. And what do you do? Sleuth?''

I was overwhelmed by simultaneous feelings of loss and triumph. Maybe I was ready at last to name my place in the world. For a moment I couldn't speak. "I order us more drinks,'' I finally said.

"You're very lucky, mind you. This has been a time in your life when everything mysteriously falls into place for you. Just consider those two men you told me about chancing to take your taxi. That was remarkable, wasn't it? Or you and poor Mr. Current both arriving on Jackson Street that night. It's as if destiny had been your manifest companion.''

"I have been lucky,'' I acknowledged. "I'm still being lucky.''

"And you're very American.''

"What does that mean, Jessica? How do you see us?''

"Well, do you know what it said on the side of a concrete mixer I saw the other day? It said, 'Find a need and fill it.' Don't you think that's the silliest thing you've ever heard? An Englishman would. But that's what America is about, that's its business, the source of its energy and vitality. Englishmen are what their grandfathers were and their grandchildren will be. Americans seem always to be busy recreating themselves in their platonic images. Mind you,'' she added, "I only arrived here last month.'' She laughed in her infectious way and turned her bracelets.

"You like it?''

"I'm exhilarated.''

"How long will you be staying?''

"The grant position ends in June.''

"And then?''

"Oh, it's far too early to say. I shall probably go home.

I miss England, I miss many familiar things, the Sussex Downs where I walk, talking to my husband, familiar things are so necessary to being able to take one's bearings.''

''You're married?'' My face must have shown how that made me feel.

''You're disappointed,'' she said. ''Does that make a difference to you? It needn't do, not as far as I'm concerned. I am here and he is there and that's the way we live our lives.''

''It matters a great deal to me. I want to see you again, do you understand?''

''Of course. It will sort itself out. You'll do what you must do. I hope you decide to see me again, I'd like it if you did.''

We came outside the restaurant to find the streets glistening with rain, rain that was still falling softly and steadily. The gentle spray of the first rain in months felt wonderful against my face, and when we reached Berkeley I suggested a walk along the pier. It was deserted except for a Vietnamese family with a flock of kids who still had their crab pots in the water and two elderly black gents sitting in lawn chairs with poles in the water and a gallon jug in a brown bag between them. They wished us a ''Good evening.'' Jessica Gage and I walked in companionable silence. On the Bridge a steady chainlink of car headlights pointed west toward San Francisco along the upper span as if seeking the greater force of illumination. Through the mist you could make out the city shimmering like some enchanted kingdom where gaiety and joy were meant to be.

Her house was in the hills. She asked me in for a drink. After a while I sensed it was time to leave and she walked with me to my car. She leaned in the window as I started up the motor, resting on her elbows. Her face was close to mine. No single feature in it was classically pretty but it was alive, unhidden, happy, and strangely, achingly familiar. We were looking at each other from inches apart, examining each other with passionate particularity. Everything receded into some unnoticed distance, the beautiful beckoning city, the house and the trees and the throb of the car's engine, everything but our two faces and a feeling of dreamy clarity, of knowing the place even though it was somewhere I had never traveled. Without a word she turned and went up the path toward her house. The door closed behind her.

I lit a cigarette and dropped the car into gear and started to zigzag down the slippery hill, its pavement made treacherously oily by the first rain. I drove very carefully down the hill and out along the boulevard until I finally reached the Bridge and became one more link in the chain of headlights drawing closer by the moment to the enchanted city that disappeared once you reached it.

ABOUT THE AUTHOR

MIKE WEISS won the 1984 Edgar Award for best fact crime book of the year for his nonfiction book, DOUBLE PLAY: THE SAN FRANCISCO CITY HALL KILLINGS. His articles have appeared in numerous publications including *Esquire*, *The Village Voice*, and *Rolling Stone*. He, his wife, and their children live in San Francisco and on the south coast of England.